MENACING MANOR

MENACING MANOR

The Sinister Summer Series

KIERSTEN WHITE

DELACORTE PRESS

Text copyright © 2023 by Kiersten Brazier
Jacket art copyright © 2023 by Hannah Peck

All rights reserved. Published in the United States by Delacorte Press,
an imprint of Random House Children's Books,
a division of Penguin Random House LLC, New York.

Delacorte Press is a registered trademark and the colophon
is a trademark of Penguin Random House LLC.

rhcbooks.com

Educators and librarians, for a variety of teaching tools,
visit us at RHTeachersLibrarians.com

Library of Congress Cataloging-in-Publication Data
Names: White, Kiersten, author.
Title: Menacing manor / Kiersten White.
Description: First edition. | New York : Delacorte Press, [2023] | Series: The sinister
summer series ; book 4 | Audience: Ages 8–12 years. | Summary: Twins Theo and
Alexander, their older sister Wil, and five new friends find themselves at an electrifying
manor run by Mister Frank and Dr. Stein.
Identifiers: LCCN 2022017069 (print) | LCCN 2022017070 (ebook) |
ISBN 978-0-593-57001-2 (hardcover) | ISBN 978-0-593-57002-9 (library binding) |
ISBN 978-0-593-57003-6 (ebook) | ISBN 978-0-593-70535-3 (int'l. ed.) |
ISBN 978-0-593-57004-3 (paperback)
Subjects: CYAC: Brothers and sisters—Fiction. | Twins—Fiction. | Electricity—Fiction. |
Mystery and detective stories. | LCGFT: Detective and mystery fiction. | Novels.
Classification: LCC PZ7.W583764 Me 2023 (print) | LCC PZ7.W583764 (ebook) |
DDC [Fic]—dc23

Printed in the United States of America
10 9 8 7 6 5 4 3 2 1
First Edition

To my inspiration for this whole series:
Ezra and his closet full of cheerful skeletons

*T*hey barely found the turnoff for the sea caves path. Alexander didn't look at the sign warning them to absolutely not go that way. He was too worried he'd agree with the sign if he read it again, and lose all the courage he was trying so hard to hold on to.

Even though it was low tide, the waves were closer to the cliff than he wanted them to be. The beach was only a narrow strip of false protection. A liminal space, Essa had called this area. Not one world, and not the other.

But how would he know where the border was in the caves, where the line of safety appeared? Where they were officially out of reach of the ocean?

"There!" Wil pointed. Sure enough, a cave entrance gaped, a circle of even darker black in the middle of the dark storm.

"The cold, unknowable sea," Alexander whispered, hoping against hope that this cave wouldn't turn into a terrible wave pool while they were still inside it.

CHAPTER ONE

The Sinister-Winterbottom children had no problems.

Their summer was rolling along as merrily as a summer could, endless days and warm nights perfumed with sunscreen and bug spray, drenched in fun and relaxation.

Theo was well on her way to precisely calloused feet that allowed her to walk on hot pavement without feeling it. Alexander was well on his way to reading through an entire library's worth of mystery novels. Wil was well on her way to doing whatever sixteen-year-old sisters do on their phones all day, but doing it while lying out on a patio lounge chair instead of holed up in her bedroom. And they were all fueled by a steady supply of perfectly baked cookies and the occasional robot-battle break supplied by their parents.

Yes, nothing had gone wrong. No one was scared or worried. Their parents were exactly how parents should be during the summertime: there when you needed them for a meal or scraped knee or library run or movie night, and otherwise minding their own business as you minded your own absolutely delicious lack of business.

"No." Alexander sighed and opened his eyes. It was too absurd to imagine. If he was going to fantasize a different summer for them, he should have given Theo wings. She'd always wanted wings, while Alexander was happy to stay on the ground. There were more than enough things for him to worry about down here; he didn't want to have to start thinking of all the bad things that could happen if he added soaring through the skies to his daily activities. Territorial birds, flying through swarms of bees, collisions with drones, air sickness. See, there he was, already afraid of what could happen in a scenario he would literally never be in.

"No, what?" Theo asked. She was hunched over the pile of locked books. Seven books, to be exact, with seven family names on them. Each with a tiny, perfect, unpick-able lock. But she *would* defeat these locks. When Theo set her mind to something, her focus and determination were fearsome to behold.

"I was trying to imagine us into a normal summer."

While Alexander was worried, Theo was mad. Along with Wil, they were crammed into a van with five new friends: Edgar Widow from Fathoms of Fun, Lucy and Mina Blood from the Sanguine Spa, Quincy Graves from Texas, and Henry Hyde from Camp Creek (who was only sort of their friend since he wasn't very friendly). The aggressively borrowed vehicle bumped and squeaked and grumbled down dark roads as they left Dr. Jay and her terrible braindyeing, and Edgaren't and his terrible Edgaren'tness behind.

They had also left the keys to these books behind, in the clutches of Edgaren't. It was all aggravating, which was a type of annoying that was so annoying it made you angry.

Theo imagined wings for herself, pictured soaring above the van, looping through the skies. Looking for threats and handily defeating them. She couldn't hold on to the fantasy, though, any more than Alexander could hold on to a dream of a normal summer.

"Yeah, no," she sighed, and went back to scratching at the locks with her tools from the ceramic building at Camp Creek. There were two long, hooky metal things for scraping pots, and one narrow wooden stick thing for, well, she wasn't sure. The tools had worked great for picking door locks, and even drawer locks, but these book locks were itty bitty. There was no way her current tools would work, but Theo hated sitting still with nothing to do with her hands.

"Is it weird that I miss Aunt Saffronia's car?" Alexander asked. "When it wasn't disappearing around us, at least."

"I miss her house. When it actually had food for us, at least."

"I know we didn't know her well, and she's—" Alexander was about to say *a ghost*, but the words caught in his throat. The word *ghost* felt like he had swallowed a pancake with no butter or syrup on it, and it was stuck, sponged onto his insides, refusing to budge. Which was a terrible mental image. Both something being stuck in his throat, and a pancake without butter or syrup or whipped cream or jam or honey butter or apple butter or—

Alexander's stomach grumbled. "I miss the food, too,"

he said. He couldn't *believe* his last meal had been served buffet style. He missed Aunt Saffronia's clean kitchen, with its black-and-white tiles and marigold walls, where he could observe all the food-safety protocols.

He also missed the blissful innocence of not realizing their aunt Saffronia, who had been charged with taking care of them for the summer, was (a) dead, (b) had been dead the entire time, and (c) was somehow banished now, which meant she was ... deader? Or still just as dead, but unable to reach them anymore? He wasn't certain of the logistics.

But he was certain that she had been the only grown-up person—well, person-*ish*—on their side. Now they didn't have anyone in charge of them, and Alexander really, really liked people being in charge. It made him feel safe and taken care of.

Theo didn't really like people being in charge of her, but she *did* really like knowing when she was going to have her next meal. And she liked weird Aunt Saffronia. It made her sad that someone had taken their aunt away from them, when their parents had very purposefully chosen Aunt Saffronia to take care of them.

Leaving Aunt Saffronia in charge seemed like a bizarre choice, made even bizarrier (Theo knew that wasn't a word, but felt like it should be: a combination of *more bizarre* and *scarier*) knowing that Aunt Saffronia was on the wrong side of the grave to be a good babysitter. But their parents had to have summoned Aunt Saffronia for a reason. They could have left Theo and Alexander with a neighbor. Or even with Wil, though to be fair even an occasionally incorporeal ghostly babysitter still paid more attention than Wil did.

Theo's aggressively borrowed wooden tool snapped in half. She set everything aside with a huff. She had to be careful or she'd jam the locks.

Mmm, jam. Without realizing it, her mind fell into the same hungry thought spiral as Alexander's as it snagged on jam, then peanut-butter-and-jam sandwiches, then peanut butter cookies. Though the Sinister-Winterbottom twins were very different, they still managed to land on the same thoughts frequently.

Meanwhile, Quincy was filling in Mina and Lucy on what they had missed. The Blood sisters had only joined their van a couple of hours ago, and so they didn't know anything about what had happened at Camp Creek. Quincy knew all about it, since she had been braindyed, alongside Alexander. Theo had saved them, and then together they had saved the rest of the campers and counselors and escaped just in time to snag Mina and Lucy, who had been on their way to the terrible camp.

Quincy toyed with her beloved lassos while narrating the events. ". . . And that's how we discovered that all our parents went to Camp Creek together one summer, and several of them mysteriously disappeared from the camp. And they were there with Dr. Jay, Henry's aunt—"

Henry made an impolite noise from where he sat facing backward, glaring out the rear windshield. His aunt wasn't a nice person, so no one blamed him for that outburst.

"—who took over Camp Creek," Quincy continued without stopping, "and was using it to brainwash—"

"Braindye," Theo corrected her.

"—braindye children into being the same, all the while working with my uncle, who y'all knew as Van Helsing and who Edgar knew as Heathcliff and who the Sinister-Winterbottoms confusingly know as Edgaren't, and who I'm very, very, very sorry to have helped, but he was in charge of me and I really thought I was doing the right thing, and—"

Mina put a hand on Quincy's shoulder. "I understand." Mina's voice was soft and kind. "I helped the Count change the spa and take advantage of people, because

7

my parents were gone and I didn't know what else to do. Without Theo, Alexander, and Wil, I might still be helping him try to trick guests into participating in his health-shakes scheme."

"And I didn't stand up to the woman pretending to be my aunt Widow at the water park," Edgar added from the driver's seat, where he steered the aggressively borrowed van through the night. "I couldn't understand why she was doing what she was doing, but I didn't feel like I had enough power to disagree with her. Without Theo, Alexander, and Wil, I might still be under the Cold, Unknowable Sea, trying to convince my uncle to come out, with the imposter Mrs. Widow destroying everything above us."

"And I hid under cabins and stole food from trash cans," Henry said, his pug nose wrinkled up like he wanted to growl at them, "none of which I regret because I wanted to do it! And I always knew my aunt was full of baloney, and not the fresh kind off the top of the trash can, but the rotten, moldy kind at the bottom, and I didn't need any of you to tell me that!" He took a deep breath. "Sorry. I get mad when I think about her. And I guess it *is* because of Theo, Alexander, and Wil that I was able to stand up to her and get away from the camp." That last part came out in a grumbled rush, as though he couldn't quite stop being angry long enough to be grateful. Sometimes, people got so used to feeling one way, even when they didn't have to feel that way anymore, it was their default reaction. Like when your glass of water is on one side of your bed, and you reach for it automatically, even if it's been moved by the ghost that occasionally haunts your room and rearranges your toys.

"Theo still hasn't guessed my sixth-favorite animal," tiny Lucy whispered, wanting to be part of the conversation.

Theo ran her hands through her always-wild hair. "Don't remind me!" It would bother her for the rest of her life that she hadn't won that game with Lucy, and yet, somehow, the braindyed counselors and campers of Camp Creek had managed to guess her own sixth-favorite animal.

"Anyway," Quincy said, her comforting Texan drawl back in place now that her brain had been freed of dye, "that's what happened. Plus, we found all these books with our family names on them. We had the keys but no books, and now we have the books, but no keys."

"But now that we have the Blood sisters with us," Edgar said, "we have almost all the families whose names are on the books."

"Sinister, Blood, Widow, Graves, Hyde, Stein, and Siren," Theo listed off, tracing the names on the covers of the books. "So we're going to find the last two families, the Steins and the Sirens, to see if they also have missing parents. Then we can figure out how we're connected, where our parents are, and what happened during their summer at Camp Creek all those years ago."

"Also, we found out Aunt Saffronia is a ghost," Alexander added.

"Oh my," Mina said, aghast. "I suppose that was a surprise!"

Wil shrugged. "Not if you were paying attention." Rodrigo's screen glowed blue, illuminating her with its cool light. "We should be at Stein Manor soon. And then the *real* work begins."

Through the windows, Alexander saw the first flash of dawn. Then he realized it was actually lightning raging along the distant horizon. They were, of course, heading straight toward it.

"Here we go again," Alexander whispered.

"We've got this. And each other." Theo meant it.

She'd had to navigate Camp Creek without Alexander, and she never wanted to face something without him again. As different as they were, Theo knew now that she depended on Alexander's insight and caution as much as he depended on her gumption and bravery.

"Always each other," Wil added from the front seat, surprising them both that she was listening. The three Sinister-Winterbottoms watched together as they barreled through the long, dark night, surrounded by friends, ready to be swallowed by a storm.

CHAPTER TWO

"It's a sign!" Quincy shouted.

Alexander agreed that the storm raging around them, with flashes of lightning, crashes of thunder, lashes of rain, and clouds so dark it barely seemed like morning, was most definitely a sign. An ominous one, telling them that they were not fleeing the storm but rather driving straight into it.

But then he realized Quincy meant a literal sign. Edgar braked, squealing to a stop in front of a green-and-black sign with stately letters. It read:

Frank and Stein Bed-and-Breakfast

"Breakfast!" Theo pumped a triumphant fist in the air.

"Keep reading," Alexander said, his own hopes washed away like the torrents of water pouring down the sign, taking flecks of paint with them.

"*Coming soon.*" Theo's stomach echoed her grumbling tone.

"There's another sign." Edgar eased the van forward. This sign was less stately and imposing. It was carved with stars and lightning bolts, and read:

Stein Manor Science Camp: Join us for an electrifying experience!

"Well, that's something, at least. The science summer camp is open." Alexander was trying to be hopeful, though it was difficult in their current circumstances. The windshield wipers were wiping so fast they blurred. It was like driving through a waterfall.

"And we need a Stein, so we ought to be able to find one there." Theo pointed to the Stein book.

"Camp doesn't start until ten a.m.," Wil said, scrolling through the website on her phone. "And it's not an overnight camp; it's a weeklong day camp."

"That's good." Alexander had had enough of sleeping over in strange places. First the Sanguine Spa, where his dreams had been haunted by Lucy—who was sitting in the middle of the van, lest any stray rays of sunshine managed to pierce the heavy clouds and hit her, triggering her allergy to light—and then Camp Creek, where he couldn't remember his dreams because he hadn't been himself.

"It's not good," Theo said. "Where will we sleep? We can't live in this van for a week."

"Maybe we'll go in and immediately find all the answers we need and be on our way to finding our parents by lunchtime?" Alexander tried to sound confident, but it came out as a desperate question. The silence that greeted him was enough answer that no one thought such an outcome was likely.

Edgar continued creeping forward, the road more of a river at this point. "There's the turnoff for the manor. I suppose we could go park and wait for it to open, though it'll be a few hours."

"What's that?" Lucy pointed. It was still too dark to see well, but Lucy had no problem piercing the gloom. Edgar inched the van forward, and sure enough, there was another turnoff and yet another sign.

"*Salty Seacliff Campgrounds,*" Wil read. She looked it up on Rodrigo. "We can park here. There are bathrooms and—"

"Good enough for me!" Quincy shouted. Everyone

agreed. Once someone said the word *bathroom* out loud, everyone in the van realized they very much needed to visit one. Edgar turned in, and they bumped and twisted and sloshed their way along the narrow road. It zigged and then zagged, gradually sloping down and ending in a parking lot with a small restroom building.

There were no other cars or signs of campers. Apparently, no one looked at this weather and thought, *Camping on the beach!* Which was reasonable. Alexander wished he could be one of the many people not here at the moment.

A small beach was carved out of the looming cliffs on either side and served as the camping space. Waves crashed, pounding with white froth onto the dark gray rocky shore. The spots for tents were impossible to see through the storm. It was hardly an ideal vacation destination right now, unless your ideal vacation revolved around being cold and wet and potentially swept out to sea in nothing but your sleeping bag.

"Let's make a plan," Wil said.

"In case of tsunamis?" Alexander asked, because that was what he was thinking about.

"No, I mean a plan for what we'll do when we go to the manor," Wil said. "No more everyone having their own plans and getting in each other's way."

"That wasn't my fault," Theo snapped. "You were acting completely braindyed. And before that, at the spa, you were acting totally vampiric. And before that, at the water park, you were acting one hundred percent oblivious to the mystery we were in the middle of."

"I know," Wil answered, turning around and actually looking at her sister. "We could have been helping each other instead of getting in each other's ways. That's why, this time, we're *all* in on the plan from the get-go. No more trying to protect you just because you're younger. This summer has affected all of us, and we're going to get through it together."

Theo gave Wil a grudging smile, and Wil winked one big brown eye at her. "Besides," Wil continued, "it's more efficient than all of us separately breaking into the same rooms looking for the same things."

"If we're going to be devious, we may as well be efficiently devious," Theo agreed.

"I'd rather us not have to be devious at all." Alexander was already feeling that special anxious tightness in his chest, and his stomach hurt now from stress more than hunger.

Theo patted his shoulder. "I'll also make a tsunami plan with you, just in case." She knew it would help him feel better. Alexander liked to feel in control, and part of how he did that was having plans for any possible scenario. Theo liked adventure, which meant she didn't need to feel in control, because she felt capable of facing anything that might come up. Including a tsunami. She pictured herself riding a tsunami on a surfboard, scooping up Alexander, and depositing him safely on top of the cliff. She didn't tell him that was her plan, though, because he definitely wouldn't think it sounded exciting or cool.

"I understand, Alexander," Mina said. "We'd all rather we didn't have to be devious." Her sweet smile was reassuring. Or at least it would have been reassuring, had Alexander not been harboring an intensely awkward crush on her. Her smile made his stomach hurt even more. He blushed furiously and looked back at Wil.

Henry folded his arms crossly. "Speak for yourselves; I like being devious."

Alexander clung to the hope of a plan making everything easier, much like he was planning on running up the road and clinging to a tree in case of a tsunami. "So, we go in and try to talk to V. Stein, who was in the camp photo with our parents."

Wil nodded. "And if it's not him in charge, we'll be wary." *Wary* was like *beware*: be wary and watch for trouble or threats. Which, given the summer they'd had so far, was a reasonable way to be. And how Alexander always was.

"We'll be extra wary," Theo agreed. "The wariest. Because every place we've been to so far, the adult in charge has been on Edgaren't's side. We won't be caught off guard this time."

Edgar nodded. "Yes! Very smart. If it's not V. Stein who greets us, we'll sign up for the day camp. That way, we'll have a full week to snoop and try to find answers."

"I don't want to do science camp!" Henry grouched. "It sounds nerdy, and I'm not a nerd!"

"A nerd is someone who cares a lot about things that interest them," Theo said, glaring back at him. "So really, nerds are the happiest people around."

"You can't make me be happy!"

"Obviously." Theo rolled her eyes. "But what *is* science camp?" Theo wouldn't admit to agreeing with Henry, but it did sound kind of boring. Like doing extra school during the summer.

Wil scrolled through the website. "Building machines. Coding. A space unit. Oceanography. A mad-scientist chemistry lab."

"That's what science camp is? It sounds awesome."

Theo folded her arms, almost as angry as Henry now. Another super-fun summer activity, and they had to be spies and gather information instead of enjoying it. She didn't know whether she hoped they'd find this V. Stein immediately and get their answers, or that they'd have to stay and do all the activities.

Alexander knew exactly what he hoped: quick answers and a quicker exit. But even he had to admit the idea of a science day camp was intriguing. Under other circumstances—circumstances that involved his parents dropping him off and picking him up each day—he would probably even sign up, which was saying something.

"After we know what we're getting into, we'll make a more specific plan," Wil said, putting Rodrigo in her pocket. "There will be something for everyone to do."

"Oh, good," Mina said. "I like being useful."

"I like spying," Lucy said.

"I like organizing and herding people," Quincy said.

"I like Wil—" Edgar coughed. "I mean, I like doing what Wil needs me to."

"I don't like anything, and none of you can make me!" Henry shouted. Alexander patted his arm to remind Henry that he was safe and among friends. Henry took a deep breath. "But I'll help."

"I like solving mysteries with my brother," Theo said, nudging Alexander with her shoulder. He nudged her back. Things were still bad and scary and stressful, but knowing Theo was at his side made his stomach hurt a little less.

"I like taking care of my family," Alexander said. That was who he was. For a little while, he had been a different person at Camp Creek. It had been easier in a lot of ways, but he was glad to be back to himself, worry and tight chest and hurting stomach and all. No one could look after Wil and Theo and their friends better than he could. He straightened his shoulders and nodded to himself. Whatever was waiting for them at Stein Manor, he would face it.

"I like using the restroom when I don't have to risk getting Rodrigo soaked just to get to it," Wil said with a sigh, staring out the watery window.

Henry threw open the van door. "Last one there is a rotten egg! Actually, everyone there is a rotten egg except me!" He sprinted across the parking lot, dashing for the cover of the building.

As the rest of them tumbled out of the van after him, Theo and Alexander held back.

"Look," Alexander said, pointing. Through the pouring

rain, perched high up on a gray rocky cliff looming over the beach, they saw a building. It wasn't as large as the Sanguine Spa, but it was no normal house, either. Three stories high, the same dark gray as the cliffs it perched on, with a sharply pointed roof and a single burning light behind one tall window. The one light was like a cyclops' eye, keeping a menacing watch on the ocean below.

"Stein Manor," Theo whispered.

A percussive boom of thunder so loud it threw them back into the van cracked as the manor was struck by lightning.

CHAPTER
THREE

Alexander blinked rapidly, trying to get rid of the bolt of lightning's glowing afterimage.

"Are you okay?" Alexander mouthed.

"What?" Theo shouted, but no sound came out. "I don't think we can hear each other!" she yelled. She couldn't hear *anything*, not the pounding ocean waves or the pouring rain.

Alexander shook his head, putting his hands over his ears. Gradually, like he was underwater, sounds started coming back until at last he could hear normally.

"That was—" he started.

"That was—" Theo continued.

"That was—" he said, then shook his head. "Whoa."

"Yes. That was whoa," Theo agreed. She looked up slowly, expecting the manor to be exploded into a thousand gray pieces, or at the very least a burning inferno. She didn't want to see the destruction, but she had to know how bad it was.

"Whoa?" she whispered. The manor was still completely intact. At the peak of its pointy roof was a metal pole. They hadn't seen it before because of the gray-on-gray-on-gray colors of the manor against the stormy sky and rocky cliff. The pole was only visible now because it was glowing white hot. Theo could almost hear the rain sizzling against it.

Even stranger, not only was the manor still completely intact, but it was brilliantly illuminated. All the windows had blazed to life, yellow light shining out. Instead of looking welcoming, though, now it seemed like the manor had even more eyes than before. Less a Cyclops, which was a creature with one head and one eye who liked to eat people, and more a Hydra, which was a creature with many heads and many eyes, who also liked to eat people.

"I'm still hungry," Theo grumbled. She was not a creature who ate people, but if she got much hungrier, she might consider it.

"Do you think the lightning strike woke them up?" Alexander asked.

"I don't know how anyone could have slept through that. But how did they get all the lights on so quickly?"

Alexander shrugged. "Maybe there are a lot of people there. Maybe the sign was wrong, and the bed-and-breakfast isn't coming soon, but has already come?"

"Maybe." They'd find out soon enough. Theo did like the idea of both beds and breakfasts, even more than science camp. Alexander liked both beds and breakfasts, and he also liked the idea that there would be many grown-ups there in case things got scary.

Still shaking her head to get the last lingering effects of the thunder out of her ears, Theo took advantage of the restrooms. They smelled like cleaning chemicals and cold, damp stone, but at least they weren't terrifying. And, somehow, there was a single bee buzzing frantically around. Perhaps it was a requirement of any outdoor restroom. As soon as they were built, the ceremonial bee was unleashed, to forever buzz and make using the bathroom slightly more tense.

Trying not to think of the restroom bee or toilet alligators, Alexander rushed back into the van. Everyone was crammed in, damp, hungry, and more than a little cross on account of the lack of sleep.

"Just three more hours until the camp opens," Edgar said, trying to sound cheerful, but sounding more like he was announcing three hours until the start of the test they had all forgotten to study for.

"No!" Wil gasped in agony.

"What's wrong?" Alexander asked, panicking.

"There's no way Rodrigo's battery will last another three hours, but I can't use the van charger if the van isn't running! And we can't waste the gas to keep it running. This is a disaster."

"Speaking of the van," Mina said thoughtfully, "we should leave it here."

"What? Why?" Henry folded his arms. "It's mine!"

"It's got Camp Creek written in huge letters along the side," Theo said. It was pretty obvious why Mina didn't want them to be seen in it. Edgaren't and Dr. Jay would be on the lookout for the van, and anyone working with them would recognize it, too.

"We need fake names," Alexander said, surprising everyone. He was a very honest kid and hated any sort of lie. But he knew who they were dealing with. Edgaren't was a liar and a cheater, willing to do anything to get what he wanted. Alexander had read a great many mystery and detective novels. He knew when dealing with villains, sometimes you had to pretend, misdirect, and trick people in order to save the day.

"Fake names?" Mina asked. She was still wearing her uniform from the Sanguine Spa, which was a long-sleeved blouse, a vest, and a huge poufy skirt. The skirt—black, with tiny purple pinstripes—was taking up a lot of space on the van seat. Lucy was curled up, using its poofs like a nest.

"The people working for Edgaren't don't usually recognize us on sight," Alexander said. "They only recognize our names. That's why the Count didn't know we were the kids he had been told to look for—he thought our last name was Swinterbottom."

Henry snickered from the back. "*Swinterbottom.*"

"Perhaps Quincy, Henry, and I can pretend to be siblings?" Edgar said, using his fingers to comb his thick black hair back from his forehead where the rain had plastered it. "That way, it'll make more sense that we're all together. We can say our family is old friends with your families. Which isn't a lie, apparently."

"Lucy and I will be your cousins," Mina said to the Sinister-Winterbottoms.

"Eurttons and Ekafs," Alexander said.

"Did the lightning hit your brother?" Henry asked Theo.

Alexander smiled. "Eurtton—Not True. And Efak—Fake. So even when we give false names, we're telling the truth, in a way."

Theo cackled. "I like that. I'm going to use that from now on when I lie—if I sneakily tell someone that I'm lying, then I'm telling the truth about lying, and it doesn't really count, does it?"

"I am quite sure it still counts," Alexander said.

"What about first names?" Edgar asked.

"I could be Dora." Theo wrinkled her nose. She didn't like it, but it was the other half of Theodora, her full name. "Alexander could be Xander, and Wil could be . . ."

"Mina," Wil said, smiling ruefully. Her full name was Wilhelmina. "That seems like it'll be confusing." Mina laughed and nodded.

"Wil-o'-the-Wisp?" Alexander suggested. Wil had never explained why she answered the phone that way, or who she had been threatening, or why she had a fake

27

burner phone in addition to Rodrigo. He wanted to ask her again, but before he could, she nodded.

"Willow works."

"We'll be Nina and Susy," Mina said. "That way if anyone messes up, it sounds close enough that we can cover." She put a hand on Lucy's back. The little girl was snoring softly. Her lips were firmly shut, though, so Theo couldn't see whether or not she actually had fangs.

Theo had never met a more frustrating child than Lucy Blood. But only because she had never met herself, and any adult who knew Theo would tell you in either exhaustion or affection that she was extremely frustrating.

It wasn't such a bad thing to frustrate adults, though. Theo knew that now, after having successfully frustrated Dr. Jay's plans to make every child act exactly the same. She didn't have to be the same as every other kid. She just had to be the best version of herself, which was something she was working on.

"I'm not changing my name!" Henry shouted. Then his tone abruptly softened. "Oh, wait, can I go by my nickname? It's Scooter."

"Who calls you Scooter?" Quincy asked.

"No one, but I'd really like people to start." Henry sounded more hopeful than angry for once.

"Scooter it is," Quincy declared.

In the end, they settled on their disguises—Alexander preferred to think of them as disguises rather than lies. Attending science camp would be Willow, Xander, and Dora Eurtton, with their cousins Nina and Susy Eurtton, and their longtime family friends, siblings Lacey (since it was sort of like rope, Quincy liked it), Scooter, and Poe Efak. Edgar put on the name like he'd put on a three-piece suit and a neckerchief. It fit him, oddly enough.

"Why Poe?" Theo asked.

"It just came to me, while I pondered, weak and weary. Is anyone else starving?" Edgar tapped on the dashboard clock as though he could make time speed up that way.

"I can't sit in this van anymore." Theo threw the door open. The rain had turned into a complaining drizzle, like the sky was whining sullenly but couldn't work itself up to a full fit anymore. "Let's get walking to the manor. We know they're awake now. Maybe they'll let us in early."

"And let me charge my phone," Wil said, stroking the screen.

Theo shoved the family books under the seat, hiding them from sight. She hated to be separated from them, but couldn't very well show up lugging around seven books with all their names on the covers if they were hoping to stay sneaky.

"Is it too sunny for Lucy?" Alexander asked, worried about the strange little girl and her allergy to sunlight.

Henry dug in the back behind the seat, shifting aside their luggage. "Here." He held out a poncho. "Like a portable tent."

"Thank you," Mina said. "That was really kind of you."

Henry ducked his head. He wasn't the type of child who people thanked or praised, and, much like he didn't know how to react to things except by being angry, he didn't know how to accept gratitude. "It's not a big deal."

"It is to me." Mina woke Lucy and helped her into the poncho; then they all climbed out of the van and waited while Edgar dutifully locked it. They might have aggressively borrowed it from Camp Creek, but they didn't want anyone to aggressively borrow it from them.

"What will we do if we don't find V. Stein right away? We can sign up for the day camp, but what about the nights?" Alexander kept thinking of his own bed and how much he missed it.

"There are tents and gear in the back of the van," Henry said. "My dad and I—" He broke off with an angry scowl.

It was strange for Theo, seeing someone else who became angry instead of sad. She knew exactly how he was feeling, thinking of his dad, the person who understood him best, who loved him best. Who was gone, and none of them knew where, or why.

"That's awesome, Henry," Theo said, not wanting him to dwell on those sad-angry feelings. "Or should I say, Scooter. You're really saving the day around here."

Henry stood a little straighter, his scowl softening. "I am!"

"So should we walk back up the road and then find the other turnoff?" Alexander asked. He wasn't looking forward to it. The road was full of potholes, which, after so much rain, were more like tiny swimming pools lying in wait to soak his unsuspecting shoes.

There are many miserable things in life. Pop quizzes. Showing up fifteen minutes early for a doctor's appointment you don't even want to go to and then having to wait another thirty minutes to be seen. Being stuck in a room while someone watches golf on TV. Inching down a waterslide designed for rafts and not swimsuited bottoms. Anything with raisins in it.

But spending the day in wet tennis shoes—and,

worse, taking off wet tennis shoes at the end of the day— was right up there with all of them. *And* it made raisins of toes, just to add insult to injury.

"Look!" Theo and Quincy pointed at the same time. Zigzagging up the side of the cliff, leading straight from the campgrounds to the manor, was a pathway carved into the rock. It looked wet and slippery and decidedly treacherous.

Alexander revised his list of miserable things, putting *getting your shoes soaked while hiking up a scary pathway along a seaside cliff with no guardrails* right at the tippy top.

CHAPTER FOUR

Theo looked at the path carved into the side of the cliff. And, as suddenly as the lights had gone on in the manor above them, she saw everything that was wrong with the trail. They'd get wet. If an impossibly large wave came, it might smack right into them and wash them away without any opportunity for her to dashingly surf them to safety. And there were no guardrails.

Theo's efforts to be cautious at Camp Creek really had changed her. "We can take the road," she said. "It's less treacherous."

"No," Alexander said. "We should take this path."

33

Theo didn't know which was more surprising—that she was being cautious, or that Alexander wasn't.

He shook his head at her questioning glance. "It'll look suspicious if we show up on the doorstep of the manor without a car or a grown-up. If we come from the campground, we can tell them we're staying here with our families. Which is sort of true, for most of us. But it also implies we're here with adults, which is not true."

Wil nodded approvingly. "You know, you're pretty good at this sneaking thing."

"Very clever!" Mina agreed.

Alexander tried not to blush, both from the compliments and also from embarrassment that he was, in fact, good at being sneaky. "When you think about things from every possible angle, you see a lot of opportunities." Usually what he saw were opportunities to get hurt or humiliated, but he also saw opportunities to avoid those things. And, in this case, to avoid suspicion. It was his way of protecting his sisters and friends. He still didn't like that it involved tricking other people, but he could accept that sometimes it was necessary. Especially when Edgaren't was involved.

Everyone buddied up to scale the cliff path. Phone-staring Wil and Wil-steering Edgar went in the lead, followed by skirt-swishing Mina and tent-wearing Lucy,

34

rope-twirling Quincy and foot-stomping Henry, and finally stomach-grumbling Theo and stomach-hurting Alexander.

Though Alexander and even Theo had worried the stairs carved into the sea cliff would be slick and slimy, they were actually porous and jagged. Their shoes gripped the wet steps easily.

"This isn't as bad as I thought it would be," Alexander said, then immediately regretted saying it out loud. It felt like a dare to the universe to make it worse. The path might not have been slippery and treacherous, but the noise of the waves crashing against the cliff side below them, the knowledge that there was nothing to the side of them but a sheer drop into the frigid ocean, and the fear of what they were climbing toward were all more than scary enough for him.

"Look!" Theo pointed. A section of the trail branched off. The others had continued upward without noticing. But the offshoot of the trail went downward.

Alexander leaned closer to the cliff face. There, carved into the stone, was a sign. He read it. *"Trail to sea caves. Warning! Do not enter! Danger!"* Alexander frowned.

"Why have a way down at all if it's so dangerous?" Theo scoffed. "They could have blocked it off."

"Do you think the sea caves are anything like the Cold, Unknowable Sea?" Alexander peered down the sea cave trail, but it zagged sharply and he couldn't see more than a few feet along it.

"And if we went in them, we'd find a lovely sitting room with Mr. Widow waiting to serve us tea." Theo snorted a laugh.

"Or they'd be like the tunnels at the Sanguine Spa and we'd find a whole colony of vampire bats."

"Or they'd be like the tunnels at Camp Creek and we'd find—"

Alexander continued. "An arrow pointing the opposite way we went, where maybe we would have found answers." He was still haunted by that moment in the tunnels beneath the camp, where they had found their mother's initials next to an arrow and an invitation to come find her. He knew, logically, that it had been carved when his mother was a teenager—if it had been his mother who had carved it at all. But he had felt so strongly that they should have gone that direction. He hadn't listened to himself, though. He had let the others make the decision.

Theo changed the subject, sensing that Alexander was upset. She was getting better at acknowledging other people's feelings. Especially when the other people in question was Alexander. "We sure do find a lot of tunnels."

"Secret passages."

"Secret libraries."

"Secret storage spaces."

Theo laughed. "It's never really a storage space! Come on." She gave one last lingering look at the forbidden path. The hive of bees that lived inside her and flared to life when she was upset or bored or confused was mostly quiet. After all, she had a clear course of action for the morning. But she could tell they wanted to explore the off-limits sea caves, too.

She wasn't going to listen to them. There was a difference between being brave and being reckless, and Theo Sinister-Winterbottom was getting very, very good at being reckful.

Alexander had no desire whatsoever to go down that other path. He hated that it was even there at all. If a path to sea caves existed, it felt inevitable that someone would take it. It sure wouldn't be him, though.

He and Theo continued their trek upward toward the manor, catching the others at the top. The grounds of the Sanguine Spa were carefully cultivated, with wide, grassy fields for running on, a hedge maze for racing through, a ropes course for climbing up, and a pool for relaxing in. The grounds of Stein Manor, however, were almost nonexistent. The manor itself had been built at the very edge of the cliff, like it was part of the cliff itself. Alexander inched as far from the edge as he could, nudging up against the wall of the manor.

The manor had gables extending on either side, and a sharply steep roof with pointy angles. On top of the roof was the giant lightning rod stabbing upward toward the gray skies. The windows were still lit, each perfectly spaced and un-curtained, as though the house couldn't bear to close its eyes. It kept a vigilant watch on the ocean—and on the scraggly, wet, hungry group of young people staring up at it.

They made an odd crew. Mina in her flowing skirt and blouse and vest. Lucy, hidden entirely in her poncho tent. Edgar in his three-piece suit that managed to look elegant even damp and wrinkled from the rain and their long night. Wil in her black tee, black jeans, and black boots. Quincy, in her cowgirl boots and hat, with a rope twirling through the air around her. Henry, in his clothes that were still so filthy from where he had been hiding underneath the cabins at Camp Creek that it was impossible to tell if they had ever been anything other than dirt-colored. And then the twins, with their matching brown hair, matching freckles, and currently matching frowns as they wondered why someone would build a house like this. Alexander because of the obvious safety risks, and Theo because of the obvious temptation of wondering if one could cliff-dive from the roof straight into the ocean.

"Look! A back entrance," Quincy said, lassoing a welcome sign over a door they hadn't noticed yet because it was all the same wet, dark gray shade. "They must have a lot of people come up from the campground."

"Do you smell that?" Henry asked, perking up. Over the scent of salt and wet rock and the peculiarly refreshing stink of the ocean, they smelled something amazing.

They smelled *breakfast.*

All thoughts of investigating further before entering evaporated like water on hot pavement, and unlike water on the cold rock around them. They needed to get inside *now.* The doorway was recessed, the roof overhang offering some shelter from the rain that was still sullenly spitting from above. Alexander and Theo stood in the back, where they got dripped on by the edge of the overhang, meaning they were being double-soaked. Getting dripped on during rain was insulting. They were already wet; they didn't need help getting even wetter.

"It says to ring the bell for science camp," Edgar said. He put a finger against the doorbell and pushed. Instead of a polite ding, there was the sound of an actual bell clanging from deep inside the manor. It reverberated and echoed outward.

It felt like an eternity standing there getting dripped on, waiting. After a few minutes, Wil shrugged from where she was hunched over Rodrigo to protect it from the rain while tapping furiously. "Should we try ringing again?" she asked.

"Or go around to the front?" Mina suggested.

Just then, the thick wooden door swung open. It was braced with metal brackets that had rusted in the wet sea air, with dark lines tracing down from the bolts like tears or scars. It creaked as it opened, an agonized sound to accompany the agonizingly slow arc of the door as it gradually revealed a man.

At least, they were pretty sure it was a man. The lights behind him burned with brilliant warmth, which cast his body into shadow. But they didn't need to see him clearly to know that he was the largest man any of them had ever stood in front of. His shoulders filled the entirety of the door frame, and his head was so high the top of it was actually higher than the door. It made his head look oddly flattened, like it was straight across instead of domed.

He looked down at them and said nothing. Alexander had never been so intimidated in his life. Even Theo felt a little unnerved by this enormous, silent man looming in the doorway.

Wil, however, hadn't bothered to look up and therefore was not intimidated by his size because she had no idea how large he was. It was easy not to be intimidated by people when you weren't paying enough attention to care. "Mr. Stein?" she asked. "Mr. V. Stein?"

A voice rumbled free of the man's chest, like it had been caged there for decades. It was a creaky, low groan, not unlike the sound the door had made as it swung open.

"You shouldn't be here." And then he slammed the door shut in their faces.

CHAPTER
FIVE

They stood, stunned in sodden silence, staring at the slammed door.

"What do we do now?" Henry demanded. Theo had thought his hair was a muddy brown, but the rain had washed away some of his under-cabin coat of dirt to reveal hair that was dirty blond. Maybe just dirty *and* blond, though. "I'm hungry! And tired and cold and wet!"

"Do you think that was him? V. Stein?" Edgar asked.

"He told us we shouldn't be here." Alexander took a step backward. It moved him out of the water drop zone and back into the drizzle. But it also moved him closer to the edge of the cliff, so he stepped forward again. "Maybe it was a warning."

"Or a threat." Theo scowled at the closed door. She was tired of being bossed around by adults who didn't know her or care about her.

"What should we do now?" Mina asked.

To Alexander's surprise, she was looking at him when she asked. *Everyone* was looking at him—except Wil, who was looking at Rodrigo, but that was nothing new. Alexander's stomach dropped. They wanted him to plan their next move. They were trusting him. Depending on him.

"I—I'm not sure, I—"

The door swung open, this time so fast it barely creaked. Instead of the hulking man, a teenage girl stood in the doorway. Though she, too, was backlit, she seemed to glow instead of glower. She wore white pants and a white flowing shirt. Her feet were bare, and her long brown hair was pulled back in a ponytail. There was something familiar about her sweet face. Or maybe it was that they all *wanted* her face to be familiar. Wanted to know her. Wanted her to let them in and feed them.

She laughed, a sound like silverware being sorted into a drawer. "Don't mind Frank," she said. "He's not a morning person. Some would say he's barely a person at all."

"In the mornings?" Mina asked.

"Sure, or anytime. Are you here for the camp? You're very early."

"We're sorry," Alexander said.

"It was raining, and we didn't have anything else to do," Edgar said.

"We're staying down at the campground," Wil added.

"With our families!" Henry shouted, managing to sound both deeply unconvincing and also angry at the same time.

"We can come back when it's time for the day camps to start." Mina adjusted the massive poncho hiding Lucy from the nonexistent sunshine.

"No, this is perfect!" The girl stepped aside, gesturing for them to enter. "I made way too much food, and I can't try it all myself. Would you like to be my lab rats to test my creations on?"

Alexander didn't like the sound of being a lab rat, but he did like the sound of breakfast. They all liked the sound of it. And they liked the smells wafting toward them on the air even more. Salty bacon and fluffy bread and sweet syrupy goodness. Theo hadn't smelled a house this delicious all summer. A growl of her stomach told her she missed her mother's baking and cooking so much it actually hurt.

Wil gestured vaguely around herself. "I'm Willow Eurtton, those are my siblings, Dora and Xander, and my cousins, Nina and Susy. And these are our close family friends the Ekafs. Poe, Scooter, and—" Wil froze. Everyone held their breaths. Wil couldn't remember Quincy's fake name! Though Wil was a genius, even geniuses have to be paying attention in order to remember things, and Wil was nearly always distracted.

"Lacey," Quincy said at last.

Wil grimaced, glancing up apologetically. "Right. Lacey."

"So not *that* close of family friends," the teenage girl said with another silvery laugh. "That's all right, I'll try my best to remember all your names so Willow doesn't have to."

They filed in past her. The door led to a sitting room that served as the central hub of the manor. Beyond them they could see an entryway with a soaring ceiling and a cold chandelier made of brutally formed metal bars. The floor was tiled with the same stone as the beach below them, uneven and rounded beneath their feet, so walking on it made them feel slightly unsteady. There were two couches in the sitting area, both long and leather, facing each other as though in a staring contest that neither would back down from. Between the two couches was the only soft thing about the room—an ornate rug depicting soaring mountains. A fireplace dominating the wall crackled, though it did little to warm the huge room. A giant staircase leading to the second story had a balcony with metal rails. Alexander looked up and could have sworn he saw someone peering at them from behind the hallway wall, but he blinked and there was no one there. It was too dim to be certain if he had actually seen someone, anyway.

Though the walls of the manor were lined with windows, they didn't brighten the space. If anything, they made it darker and colder by reflecting the cloudy oppression of the day outside. It felt like the sea and the storm were trying to shoulder their way in.

The best feature of the room by far, though, was that the man who had told them they shouldn't be here was nowhere to be seen.

"So the grouchy guy wasn't V. Stein?" Theo asked.

Their hostess shook her head, closing the door behind them as the last of their group sloshed inside. "No, that's

Mr. Frank. Victor Stein isn't here right now. He had to go on a short trip, but he'll be back soon."

"He's not missing?" Quincy tried to sound innocently curious, her lasso forming a question mark in the air. But Quincy being sly was about as convincing as Henry trying to sound happy. Quincy talked like she was lassoing her topics and dragging information toward herself.

They were all terrible at this, Alexander realized with a sinking stomach. If this girl was the suspicious type, she'd know they were up to something.

"Missing?" The girl laughed. "Why would he be missing? Oh, did you mean missing the camp this week? Maybe. I'm not sure when he'll be back. But don't worry. I can handle you all by myself. Promise." She winked. Her eyes were hazel, and she had a smattering of freckles along the bridge of her nose.

"And you are?" Wil asked.

"Oh, right! You can call me Essa. I'm working here for the summer."

"Are you related to Victor?" Alexander asked. The rest of them were all related to someone from one of the families on the book covers. Maybe Essa was, too. Maybe Victor was missing like their parents, and she didn't know it yet. She could be the Stein they needed to add to their group! He hoped she was.

Essa shook her head. "Old family friend, like you all. Come on! We don't want things to get cold." She led them through a wooden doorway and down a hall with several closed doors. The stone floors beneath their feet were eerily silent. The manor had none of the soft, familiar sounds of a home, and they hadn't seen anyone except Essa and Mr. Frank so far.

Theo was on the lookout, ready to spring into action to protect Alexander, Wil, and their friends. But other than being cold and unwelcoming, the manor hadn't presented any threats yet. Or any answers.

Alexander, too, was on high alert. If they had decided to look for the Steins, surely Edgaren't would also figure out how to find the sixth of the seven families. In fact, not only had Edgaren't found everyone else so far, he had *beaten* the Sinister-Winterbottoms to all their destinations, or at least sent someone working for him there first. So Alexander felt confident he wasn't being unreasonable to be nervous and suspicious.

"We're following her without knowing where we're going," Alexander whispered to Theo. "She seems nice, but ..."

"But we don't know if we can trust her," Theo agreed. "For all we know, she's leading us to a dungeon, or to a surprise mean-mustache party."

"She seems familiar, though. Doesn't it feel like you already know her? I can't put my finger on it."

"Same. Maybe—"

"Welcome to my laboratory!" Essa said, her voice low and mysterious as she pushed open a door.

CHAPTER
SIX

E ssa's laboratory was not filled with beakers and
scientific instruments. No creepy glowing test
tubes, no white lab coats, no long metal tables
that were the perfect size for a body to lie on. Instead,
it was filled with stoves and a fridge, steaming pots and
pans, aprons, and long counters that were the perfect size
for a tremendous amount of food to lie on.

The kitchen was the same oppressive gray
stone as the rest of the building, but it was clean
and organized, and the sparkling counters
positively overflowed with every breakfast
goody imaginable. There was a cozy, worn

table near a window, with enough seating for all of them, but there were also stools lining the counters.

"Have at it," Essa said with a smile, gesturing to the entire kitchen.

"Electricity," Wil chirped, rushing to the counter and plugging her phone charger into an outlet there. "Whoa," she whispered. "Rodrigo's never charged this fast. This place is a dream come true."

"The real dream come true is food!" Theo sighed, overwhelmed with relief. She could keep better watch once her stomach wasn't demanding so much attention. She plopped down in front of a platter of gooey cinnamon rolls, the icing still warm and dripping over the edges.

Henry chose a plate of sausage and eggs with toast. Quincy lassoed a basket of pastries and tugged it to herself. Mina helped Lucy out of her poncho tent, and then gave her a bowl of blackberries so dark and juicy they stained the little girl's hands an alarmingly bloodlike shade.

Edgar politely inquired if there was tea. Essa helped him pour a cup while Wil perched on her stool and began eating whatever was in front of her without looking up. In this case, it was overnight French toast, drizzled with syrup, dusted with powdered sugar, and topped with freshly sliced strawberries.

"Did you make all this?" Alexander asked, taking it in. He liked to bake and cook, but he couldn't imagine doing this much in a single morning. His mom might be able to, though. She was a fiend in the kitchen, constantly testing new recipes and tweaking old ones.

"Yes," Essa answered. "Try the bread pudding." She pushed a small, warmly fragrant bowl in front of Alexander.

Now, most children will hear the term *bread pudding* and think a pudding cup filled with soggy bread and immediately say, "No, thank you." That's a perfectly fair way to react to something called bread pudding. Whoever named it really didn't think through the branding, unlike whoever named toad-in-the-hole. Toad-in-the-hole didn't sound appetizing, but it did sound *exciting*. Bread pudding sounded like standardized testing day at school. Would it kill you? No. But would it be pleasant? Absolutely not.

However, Alexander had tried enough strangely named things thanks to *The Magnificent English Confectionary Challenge* to know that bread pudding was, in fact, a deliciously comforting food. It was sweet and eggy and soft all at once. The best way he could describe warm bread pudding was like eating a really good hug.

He took a deep breath, smelling it and smiling. It made him feel safe. It made him feel like he was home again. Except . . .

"My mom makes bread pudding a lot like this, but she swirls in cream cheese and raspberries."

"Oh," Essa said, her smile freezing. "This is a very old recipe."

"She loves tinkering with recipes, always trying to make them better."

"Sometimes things are perfect just the way they are." Essa handed him a fork. He worried he had hurt her feelings, so he took a bite. It was really good, but not quite as perfect as his mom's. Still, it was wonderful to eat something warm and comforting when he was cold and nervous. He gobbled it up, and Essa's smile relaxed.

"No raisins!" Theo gave a sticky thumbs-up from where she was on her third cinnamon roll.

Essa laughed. "I'm not a monster! A baker should never use raisins when chocolate chips are right there for the taking."

"I like you," Theo mumbled around a mouthful of icing-covered deliciousness. She often spoke with her mouth full, unable to wait lest she forget what she was going to say. Everything she wanted to say always felt urgent, so she had to get it out. "How are these so good?"

"I zest the cinnamon rolls with orange, cutting through some of the sweetness with a bit of acidic tartness. Too much sugar is overwhelming. We all need some balance."

Alexander nodded thoughtfully. "Baking is like science. If you adjust the variables a little, you get something new."

"Baking *is* science," Essa said. "And it's one of our courses! What better place to be a mad scientist than in the kitchen, where your creations are not only genius but also delicious?"

Alexander felt a thrill of excitement. Experimenting in a kitchen was exactly what he wanted to do. But his thrill deflated like toad-in-the-hole pulled out of the oven too soon. The classes weren't why they were really here.

"Are there any guests at the manor?" he asked after chewing and swallowing a bite. Alexander never spoke with his mouth full. Both to be polite, and because he was afraid of choking. Everything he wanted to say always felt potentially embarrassing, so he had to think it through. "We saw the lights go on this morning."

Essa placed a perfect quiche on Edgar's plate. Theo understood the appeal of a quiche in theory, but she didn't see why anyone would choose an egg-ham-and-cheese mini pie when there were cinnamon rolls and French toast and things that required pools of syrup.

"We're not ready for guests yet," Essa said. "The bed-and-breakfast keeps getting delayed. This summer all we're doing is the science camp. But you already know that, because your parents registered you for camp this morning."

"They did?" Quincy asked, incredulous, a word that means something is either so incredible or so unlikely that you can't quite believe it. "When did they do that?"

Wil cleared her throat, sneakily waving Rodrigo. That's what she had been so intent on while they were waiting to get in.

Alexander felt tears well. For a moment there with Quincy, he had thought their parents might actually have signed them up. He missed them so much it felt like all that missing was a physical thing stuck in his throat. He swallowed hard, which made too much bread pudding go down at once.

He coughed, trying to dislodge it. Theo patted him hard on the back, which anyone who is coughing or trying to swallow can tell you is not helpful at all. Essa passed him a glass of orange juice, and he took several sips.

"Are you all right?" she asked.

He nodded, not trusting himself to speak with tears so close to the surface. Alexander never minded crying, but he didn't like crying in front of people he didn't know. It made him embarrassed, which made the tears even harder to fight off.

"Yes," Theo said brightly, trying to distract Essa and give Alexander a moment to recover from whatever was making him tear up. She knew he got embarrassed when he cried in front of strangers. "We registered first thing this morning. Our parents won't be coming in at all. They aren't available."

"That's fine," Essa said brightly, "since it's not a science camp for parents."

"How many other kids are coming?" Quincy asked, lassoing a carton of chocolate milk.

"I'm not sure." Essa tapped her fingernails, clean and trimmed and unpolished, on the counter. "Actually, I'm surprised you were able to register at all. I thought the website was down."

"It was until I fixed it," Wil muttered.

"Really?" Essa sounded delighted. "Mr. Frank is in

charge of the website, and he insisted he had no idea what was wrong with it and couldn't get it fixed. How wonderful that you did! Thank you." She set a bowl of freshly whipped cream down in front of Wil, then replaced the blackberries, which had been destroyed by Lucy. Half of them were eaten, and the other half appeared to have been drained of all their juice, their shriveled husks on the counter. Mina fussed, cleaning up after her sister.

Essa flitted around the kitchen so fast she barely seemed to touch the floor as she refilled plates and gauged reactions to the food, taking notes on what they liked. Henry had a long list of complaints, even though his plate was cleared. Once he had finally reached the end of his complaints, Essa pulled out a clipboard and set it in the center of the counter.

"Here's the signup sheet for this week's classes," she said. "Oh, silly me, I don't have a pen. I'll be right back."

She hurried out of the kitchen, humming to herself.

Everyone dropped their forks and gathered around the sheet.

"So, what do we think?" Edgar asked, sipping his tea. Only Edgar could look that cool drinking tea out of a delicate cup. Alexander thought if Edgar was a guest star on his mom's favorite show—*Harfordshropshireton*

Manor, about fancy people in an English manor that was not perched on the edge of a sea cliff like this manor, and the people who lived downstairs and did all the work so the upstairs people could continue to be fancy—he'd be some sort of lord or duke and everyone would like him and Alexander would probably dress as him for Halloween.

"I need time to work," Wil answered, nibbling on some of the undrained berries as she unplugged a somehow already fully charged Rodrigo. "I'm researching how to summon ghosts."

"How to summon ghosts?" Alexander didn't like the way his voice squeaked when he asked that. "Why?"

Wil glowered at her phone as though Rodrigo were guilty of something. "Because I want Aunt Saffronia back. They had no right to send her away. Besides, if Mom and Dad wanted us to stay with her, there's probably a reason."

Theo felt the same way, and she nodded. "Good."

Alexander nodded, too. Summoning Aunt Saffronia sounded much less scary than summoning ghosts in general.

"And we need time to snoop." Theo licked the last bits of icing off her fingers. "Maybe we can find information even without Victor Stein here. Plus, I have to find tools to pick those tiny, terrible locks. I'll bet they have loads of useful tools here for sciencey things."

"I don't know about y'all, but I think these classes look really neat." Quincy was tapping on the signup sheet. "There's baking—you'll like that, Alexander. The science of mood and aggression—it's like that one was designed for you, Henry."

Henry glowered. "It was not! I'll take it anyway, but only because I want to!"

"And here, historical theories of life and the undead." Quincy looked surprised but pleased. "I want to take that one."

"Theories of the undead?" Mina sounded worried. "That hardly seems like science. More like science fiction."

"Or horror," Alexander added. He didn't like horror one bit.

Theo did. She liked getting to feel that thrill of fright when she chose to. But she didn't really want to take that class. She had other things to do here.

Quincy twirled her lasso through the air so it looked like a question mark again. "Everything's science fiction until it becomes science fact. Look, there's a class on blood disorders and medical treatment advances. Gosh, these seem awfully advanced and also specific for a kids' day camp."

Mina grabbed the sheet and dragged it to herself, her eyes big and hungry. Alexander didn't want to be caught looking at Mina, so he looked around instead. Lucy was nowhere to be seen. Then a flash of white disappeared into one of the cupboards. Even without her network of secret passageways through the walls of the spa, Lucy wasn't going to sit and listen like a normal child.

"I say we officially do the camp," Theo said. "That gives us an excuse to be here all day, every day. Alexander and I can snoop and try to pick the locks, Wil and Edgar can research how to get Aunt Saffronia back, Quincy and Henry can keep Essa busy so she won't notice us snooping, and Mina and Lucy can be in charge of keeping an eye on Mr. Frank. I didn't like him."

"Why would we have Lucy do that?" Mina blinked in confusion.

"Where is she now?" Alexander asked, smiling.

Mina looked around. "I don't know."

"Exactly," Theo said. "No one is better at sneaking information and spying than Lucy."

"That's true," said a tiny, unseen voice from the opposite side of the kitchen.

"And you're kind and helpful, Mina," Alexander said, studiously avoiding making eye contact with her. "Plus, you know how to run a guest hotel and spa. It sounds like Mr. Frank and Mr. Stein are having trouble opening a bed-and-breakfast, so maybe you can use that as an excuse to talk to Mr. Frank. That way we'll know more about him and also track his movements."

"We can't trust *any* adults," Theo said. "Don't forget."

Alexander hated the sound of that but nodded along with the others. They had a plan now, and they were all on the same page for once. They were going to attack this manor from every angle and make it give up its secrets, one way or another.

CHAPTER
SEVEN

When Essa came back into the kitchen, Mina was already clearing up the dishes and putting away leftovers.

"You don't need to do that," Essa said. "Frank will."

"Oh, but I like to help," Mina answered with a smile. "I'd love to talk to Mr. Frank, too. I run a—" Mina paused, eyes widening. Theo made an alarmed face at her. If Mina told Essa she ran a spa hotel, it wouldn't be hard to figure out who Mina really was. "Bed-and-breakfast. The, uh, Hotel Eurtton. With my parents. So I have a lot of experience. I can chat with him about his plans, maybe offer some help or pointers."

Essa's smile got even bigger than Mina's, like they were in some sort of smile-off, each trying to outsmile the other. "I'd avoid talking to Mr. Frank if I were you. He isn't exactly friendly. Besides, you're here for science camp! Not to work."

"But I love working."

"But—"

Alexander interrupted them. "Can we see where the classes are? Or is it still too early?"

Essa turned her smile on him. "Of course." She hesitated near the bread pudding, looking down at it with a sudden scowl, like clouds passing over the sun. "Improved the recipe," she muttered. Then she shook it off, smiling once more, and led them out of the kitchen, down the hallway, and up a back set of stairs. They were narrow and tight, hidden from the rest of the house, unlike the grand soaring staircase in the middle.

"It's an old manor," Essa called over her shoulder at the procession following her. "These were the stairs the servants used so they wouldn't get in the way of the manor owners."

"Like on *Harfordshropshireton Manor!*" Alexander felt a thrill of excitement, which was instantly ruined by wishing his mother were here with him so they could pretend to be in the show. Though Stein manor in general was more dour than opulent—it looked less like a fancy wedding cake in building form like *Harfordshropshireton Manor* did and more like, well, if a bunch of rocks got together and designed a place for humans to live. But still. Alexander was certain his mother would have been as delighted by servant stairs as he was.

Theo had never watched the show. It was too boring for her brain, all those people talking about what other people were talking about, which was usually what someone thought someone else was talking about when really they had been talking about something else entirely. It was so, so much talking. No one ever blew things up, or did anything daring or adventurous. So the excitement of servant stairs was lost on her. "Why couldn't they just use the huge stairs in the center of the house?" Theo asked. It made no sense. Those stairs were more than big enough for two people to pass each other without even touching.

"Because sometimes people think they're too important to be bothered by the presence of someone they don't like to think about." Essa threw open a door, and they emerged into a large, open room. It was lined with windows so it looked like they were suspended in the stormy sky itself. Alexander walked up to one and found that he could see straight down into the ocean.

"Do you ever worry that the manor is going to . . . fall?" he asked, swallowing hard and taking a step back.

"I have too many other things to worry about," Essa said with a laugh. "Besides, it's not my manor. That's for Victor and Frank to worry about. Now, if you'll all take a seat at the periodic table." She pointed to a large rectangular table that took up much of the center of the room. It was hard to look at a boring table, though, given how much other stuff was in here. Theo's eyes were gobbling it up as fast as she had gobbled cinnamon rolls.

The walls were lined with shelves and cupboards, all filled with boxes and vials and instruments. There were beakers, and Bunsen burners, and safety goggles (Alexander liked seeing those very much), and an entire table with bits and pieces of machinery and the tools to work with them (Theo liked seeing those very much), and a long counter-height table covered with supplies that they were fairly sure existed to make the ultimate goal of all science experiments: *volcanoes*.

Scarcely able to drag herself to the one boring table, Theo sat with a huff. "Why is this the periodic table? Doesn't periodic mean only happening occasionally?

It's periodically a table, and then the rest of the time it's something else?" Actually, a table that transformed into other things could be interesting.

Essa laughed that silvery laugh. "No, silly, it's the periodic table of the elements."

Alexander saw the whole thing had been precisely carved with the periodic table of the elements, which was a way that scientists used to organize and talk about all the different materials that made up the world we live in. He was sitting in front of the section of noble gasses.

"What do you call it when you have to burp in front of friends?" Henry asked.

"No," Alexander said, refusing to play. He was not at all fond of body humor.

"What?" Theo asked, happy to play. She was quite fond of body humor.

Henry let out a large belch smelling of sausage and eggs. "Ignoble gas."

"What do you call it when a king has the toots?" Theo asked.

"Noble gas!" Henry shouted.

"Nope." Theo's eyes gleamed mischievously. "Royal fanfare." She put her hands over her mouth like playing a trumpet. "Toot, toot, TOOT!"

Henry's face warred between being angry that Theo set him up for an obvious punch line and then changed it, and being amused because it was a good joke. Alexander was doing his absolute best to ignore both of them.

Quincy, meanwhile, laughed so hard her face turned bright red. "Royal fanfare. That's what I'm going to call it from now on when I'm gassy."

"Change the subject," Wil said, looking away from Rodrigo long enough to roll her eyes.

Alexander studied the surface in front of him. He was worried there might be a test on the periodic table later, and he didn't want to be caught unprepared. It didn't seem like a summer science camp should include tests, but he wasn't willing to risk failing.

"Did you all decide what classes you'd like to take today?" Essa asked.

"Are any other kids coming?" Theo hoped there would be, because that would be more chaotic and make it easier for their group to do their own tasks.

"I'm not sure. The website wasn't working until Wil fixed it, so no one could sign up."

"Why didn't Mr. Frank fix it?" Theo felt a suspicion creeping down her back, like a spider using her spine as a ladder. "Seems weird that he wouldn't want the website up. Almost like he doesn't want kids coming here."

"It does seem like that, doesn't it!" Essa shrugged. "Ever since Victor left, things have been . . . strange. Stranger, I suppose. I don't know; it's not my job to worry about that."

Edgar cleared his throat. "Is it only you teaching? What about Mr. Frank?"

"He's . . . not good with kids."

"But you're the same age as us," Wil said, gesturing vaguely around the table to mean herself, Edgar, and Mina, the only teenagers. "It's weird that you're the camp instructor. What do you do when you aren't being all sciencey?"

"Oh, the exact same things as you, I suppose."

"So you're on your phone all the time?" Theo asked. But Essa didn't appear to have a phone at all. She glanced at Wil's phone with a suspiciously confused look.

"No. I don't trust technology. It's always changing. Things shouldn't change. People get left behind when things change."

Wil laughed. "You sound like an old person."

Essa echoed her laugh. "Well, I'm old enough to run a science camp. And I promise I do a great job. You'd much rather have my science camp than Mr. Frank's." She glanced at the door leading to the stairs, a shadow flitting across her face. Alexander followed her gaze. He couldn't see anything, but he could have sworn there was a creak on the stairway, like someone gigantic was lurking in the darkness just out of sight.

"Sure, whatever," Wil said. "Poe, Nina, and I are a little old for doing the classes, though. We want to do independent study."

Edgar nodded. "Yes. I, Poe, would like to do independent study. Is there somewhere quiet we can go?"

"With a strong Wi-Fi signal," Wil added.

Essa pointed. "Yes, of course. Through those doors, on the left, you'll find the reading room. I'm not sure how the Wi-Fi signal is. Or what it is." She giggled. "Which is why I couldn't fix the broken website. Thank goodness for you!"

Wil stood, following Edgar in the direction Essa had pointed. But she paused and dragged her eyes away from her phone, looking at Theo and Alexander.

"Be careful," Wil mouthed.

Alexander nodded, and Theo gave a thumbs-up. Theo wasn't even annoyed at the warning, because she knew now she could be careful when she really set her mind to it. It made her proud. And besides, she had Alexander with her this time, so she didn't even need to worry. He'd be careful for her.

Quincy stood. "Is that a volcano-making station? I'll bet that's very time- and labor-intensive, what with building the wire frame, making the papier-mâché, gathering all the elements for an eruption. I think Hen—Scooter and I would like to do that, and I think it'll take all day and we'll need a lot of help!" Quincy beamed, sending an exaggerated wink to Theo and Alexander.

Alexander gave her a weak smile. Theo threw her head back in exasperation. They were all so, so bad at this, and it was embarrassing.

Henry's eyes were wide, his expression almost frighteningly excited. "You mean I can make something explode? And it's *allowed?*" He pumped a fist in the air as he raced over to the table with Quincy. "It's volcano time!"

"Where is Susy?" Essa looked around the room.

"Who's Susy?" Henry asked, distracted by gathering supplies for the most volcanoiest volcano ever.

Essa's eyes narrowed in suspicion. "What do you mean, who's Susy?"

Mina stood up in a rush. Alexander froze. Theo's hand found his under the table.

They were caught.

CHAPTER EIGHT

Mina laughed, the sound awkward and forced. "Scooter, you goof. You know we call little Susan Susy for short. Honestly, I think you'd forget your own name sometimes if we didn't call you by it, Scooter Ekaf." Her smile was more like a grimace. But then it shifted into a sincere expression of worry as she looked around. "Oh, dear. Where *is* Susy?"

Alexander couldn't tell whether or not Mina was acting now. Lucy creeping around was part of the plan. But, given that it was Lucy, Alexander doubted she was actually participating in the plan. It was far more likely Lucy had decided to creep around for fun and petty theft without telling Mina.

Mina's hands fluttered around her stomach, toying with one of the dozen tiny silver buttons on her vest. She looked more at home in this spooky old manor than Essa in her cheery white clothes. "My sister has a tendency to ... wander off and hide. I'll go look for her. It will probably take a long time, so don't wait for us." Mina swished out of the room.

"Well, only you two left without anything to do." Essa sat across from Theo and Alexander. She studied their faces intently, like she was looking for something. Maybe looking for a reason why everyone here didn't seem quite settled in who they said they were. Alexander felt terrible, lying to her. She was fun and nice, and he felt safe with her.

"You know, you two seem very familiar," she said.

Alexander was surprised. "I feel the same way about you."

"Do you?" Essa tilted her head. "Strange."

"Have you met a man with small, mean eyes and a large, mean mustache?" Theo asked. She didn't mind sneaking around and fibbing, because it felt more like acting than lying, but she also liked Essa and wanted Essa to be their friend. She had to be sure that Essa didn't know Edgaren't, though.

Essa laughed. "Is that the beginning of a riddle?"

Theo shook her head. "No."

"It sounds like it could be a nursery rhyme. Like 'Do you know the muffin man?' Only in this case, 'Do you know the mustache man?' Definitely less appetizing than muffins, though. Imagine walking around with a basket of mustaches!"

"He's very unappetizing," Theo agreed. She was glad Essa didn't know who they were talking about. That meant either Edgaren't hadn't been here, or he hadn't been here recently. Theo glanced at Alexander, trying to ask a question with her eyes: should they tell her the truth?

Alexander knew he was cautious. Sometimes too cautious. But they still didn't know anything about Essa. And maybe, by telling her the truth, they'd make her summer terrible and treacherous, too. She didn't deserve that; she had nothing to do with any of their troubles. Besides which, they trusted her because she wasn't an adult. That also meant she wasn't in charge and could only help them in the way a teenager could. They already had several helpful teenagers who had no choice but to join them on this wretched summer of mysteries. No reason to bring another one in.

Alexander gave a small shake of his head.

Theo let out a frustrated puff of air, but she trusted Alexander's judgment. "I'm going to that table." She walked over to the one with all the mechanical materials. The goal was to look for tiny lockpicking tools, but Theo found herself frozen.

All the gears and wires, the soldering iron, the boxes of bits and bobs, the general organized chaos of it, reminded her of her dad's workshop. Her bees at last buzzed to angry life, swarming around, demanding she do something with her hands so she didn't have to feel what she was feeling, which was very lonely and very worried and very sad. But Theo didn't know how to feel those feelings, so they all translated into a loud, angry buzz inside her.

A hand came down gently on her shoulder, more like the memory of a touch rather than an actual touch. She looked over and was surprised to find Essa also gazing down at the table with an expression that was both angry and sad.

"I once knew a boy who loved making things," she said. "This table reminds me of him." A flash of fury lit her face but was almost immediately replaced with a hollow, sad sort of look. "I don't like this table very much. It makes me feel things I don't want to feel."

"Like what?" Theo asked.

Essa shook her head and knocked on the metal table. The sound rang out. "Sound waves are funny. We think it's loudest to shout through the air, but sometimes things that seem solid move sound much farther. Water. Metal, like the manor bell. Someone once rang a bell for me, and I swear I can still feel the vibrations, all this time later." Essa shook her head once more, coming back from whatever she was remembering. "Are you okay to work here on your own for the morning while I help with the volcanoes?"

Theo nodded. She wondered what was making Essa feel angry and sad when she looked at the table, but it was apparent the other girl wasn't going to share that with her. Theo didn't like sharing her own feelings, either.

Essa gave her a small smile. "I think we understand each other, Dora."

Theo flinched at her fake name. She didn't like lying to Essa. It felt like lying to her mom. Any time Theo tried it, as soon as the words left her mouth, she could tell her mother knew she was lying. She could see it as her mom's eyes grew soft and disappointed.

It was almost like magic, the way their mom could make Theo confess the truth simply by listening to a lie without accusing her. But before she could apologize to Essa or confess, Essa had turned and drifted back to Alexander, who was still seated at the table.

"And you," she said. "What would you like to do? Volcanoes? Independent research? Building machines with your sister? Normally we're a little more formal around here. We will be tonight for some special activities, but you all signed up so late that I wasn't prepared. Plus, Victor isn't here to run things while I help. I'm still getting used to being in charge."

Alexander bit his lip, trying to decide what to do. He looked over at Theo, who was carefully sorting through tools. She needed privacy, which meant he should get Essa out of this room. Which meant Essa couldn't be overseeing the volcano projects, so he had to give her something else to do. He doubted he could convince Henry to do something else now. The other boy was already building a frame taller than himself, intently focused.

A stroke of genius flashed, and Alexander had the perfect idea. "I was hoping for some kitchen science. Would you like to figure out my mother's bread pudding recipe together?"

Essa's face twitched. Her eyes narrowed, but then her expression smoothed like a whiteboard being wiped clean. "How about we do some different experimenting in the kitchen? Try something new for both of us."

"I saw on *The Magnificent English Confectionary Challenge* once that you can make cake in a cup in the microwave in under a minute, and I've been dying to figure out how. It looks like an actual sponge when it comes out, instead of a regular sponge cake. I wonder how it tastes?"

Essa clapped her hands. She seemed genuinely excited. "I've never heard of that! Let's go figure it out together. Scooter, Lacey, keep working on those volcano frames. I'll check in later."

Quincy's lasso somehow formed a thumbs-up in response, her attention on her own project. Henry didn't even acknowledge them.

As Alexander and Essa left the room, Theo slipped a wide variety of tools into her pockets. There were tiny screwdrivers that looked like they belonged in a dollhouse, various lengths of metal wire she could twist and bend, and even one adorably small hammer. Not because she thought it would help on the books, but because she liked it. Her tool selection didn't matter right now, anyway. Until she could get back down to the campsite and the books, she had nothing to do but snoop. And Alexander had given her the perfect opportunity. He was good at this. If she wasn't so proud of him, she might be competitively jealous.

"Distract Essa if she comes back," Theo said to Quincy and Henry. "And if she asks about me, tell her I'm studying with Wil and Edgar. Or Willow and Poe, I guess."

"We're on it!" Quincy lassoed a chair and dragged it across the room to sit on as she worked on her volcano. Henry was already standing on a chair, stretching his wire frame as high as he could. Theo had a feeling Henry wouldn't be much help today, but she knew he had had the worst summer of all of them so far, which was saying something. He deserved a little volcanic distraction.

"All right, manor. Ready or not, here I come," Theo whispered as she crept out into the hallway.

Unfortunately for her, the manor *was* ready. She hadn't made it halfway down the hall when an absolutely enormous hand came down on her shoulder.

"Stop," the creaking rumble of Frank's voice demanded.

CHAPTER NINE

Alexander was peering into cupboards. "Do you have a siphon and gas canisters? Do you know what a siphon even is? I've seen them, but I don't really understand. This seems more complicated than I was imagining. I suppose we don't have a video editor to make it all look quick and easy, like they do on *The Magnificent English Confectionary Challenge*."

"Is that your favorite show?" Essa asked.

He nodded. "One of them. I watch it with my mom, and we celebrate the finales by making an elaborate dessert."

"Mmm."

Alexander straightened and looked at Essa.

She was staring into the distance, her expression cold and troubled like the ocean beneath them. Maybe she had a bad relationship with her own mother, which made him sad. He imagined it would be difficult to have parents who weren't kind, or who didn't understand you.

"What flavor do you want?" he asked, trying to nudge her out of whatever thoughts she had gotten lost in.

Essa turned her head, focusing on him once more. "Chocolate."

"That's my mom's favorite, too," Alexander said, then wanted to slap his forehead. He kept bringing up his mom. But being in a kitchen, baking and experimenting, made him think of her. Miss her, too, even more than he had been.

This time it was Essa's turn to cheerfully redirect his thoughts. "Aha! A siphon and gas canisters!" Essa gestured triumphantly to the cupboard she was holding open. Alexander noticed small handprints, sticky with what he assumed—hoped—was red juice from the breakfast blackberries. Lucy had been there. He quickly grabbed the supplies so Essa wouldn't see the evidence of Lucy's odd habits.

"Do you know how to use them? It sounds dangerous."

Alexander frowned at the shiny metal cylinder. It had a nozzle at the top, not unlike cans of spray whipped cream. But gas canisters meant pressurization, and anything that was under intense pressure was dangerous.

"Does your mom know how to use them?" Essa had a tone in her voice that Alexander recognized, having heard it many, many times from Theo. Essa was feeling competitive.

"No."

"Good! We'll figure it out together." Essa directed Alexander to begin mixing the ingredients. She fiddled with the siphon, loading the gas canisters that would inject air into the cake batter and fizz it all up. She hummed absently as she worked.

Alexander slowed, then paused his stirring. His heart hurt. His mom had the same habit of humming and singing small snippets of songs to herself when she was focused. But he didn't want to bring it up to Essa. Maybe she'd tell him why talk of mothers made her sad. But unless she wanted to open up, he wouldn't push it.

He was good at understanding other people's emotions, because he was so constantly in tune with his own. But that also made him aware that sometimes, even when your emotions were obvious to everyone around you, you weren't ready to talk about them yet. And that was okay, too.

"So, what's Mr. Stein like?" Alexander asked instead, hoping to use this moment to gather information.

There was the smallest, faintest squeak from somewhere outside the kitchen. Alexander turned to Essa, but . . . she was gone.

Meanwhile, in the upstairs hallway, Theo let out a squeak of surprise and fear. She looked up, up, up into the distant face of Mr. Frank. He glowered down at her, his eyes deep set and such a pale blue they looked almost colorless. His hand on her shoulder felt like a sack of flour, surprisingly heavy.

"You can't be here." Mr. Frank's voice was a low rumble, like a warning of thunder on the horizon, or the promise of a train barreling down tracks toward you.

Theo was glad Alexander wasn't with her, because he'd be scared. *She* wasn't scared. She was angry. She was tired of adults she didn't trust telling her where she could and couldn't be. *Who* she could and couldn't be.

"I signed up for the science day camp," Theo said,

glaring upward. "I'm allowed to be here. Besides, I'm only looking for a bathroom."

"You and your friends need to—"

"Frank?" a sweet voice called down the hallway. Essa appeared out of nowhere, like a shooting star lighting up the night sky. "It's okay for Theo to be here. Remember what we talked about?" She spoke with a smile, but her eyes were narrowed.

Frank dropped his hand from Theo's shoulder. He mumbled something unintelligible and then lumbered down the hallway.

"Thanks." Theo let out a relieved breath.

"The bathroom is clearly marked in the central science room," Essa said, her eyes shining with amusement.

Theo wrinkled her nose. "Would you believe I . . . wanted to use a different bathroom?"

Essa laughed. "Listen. Don't mind Frank. He's an old grouch. If he tries to talk with you again, come find me and I'll sort it out. Don't listen to a word he says. Usually, Victor is here to handle him, but until he gets back, it's my job. And if you want to snoop around the manor, here's a trick: Frank's boots creak as he walks. Even when he's downstairs on the quiet stone floor you can hear him coming. It sounds like floorboards groaning.

Keep an ear out and duck into hiding if needed. Problem solved."

"You're . . . okay with me snooping?" Theo asked, incredulous.

"Oh, sure! This manor is old and cool and sort of creepy. I've done my fair share of snooping. In fact, you and I can snoop later if you're still in the mood."

"Wow, yeah. I'd like that! And I'd like to hear if you've found anything interesting." Theo loved Essa. She was funny and tough and a little bit wicked. And Theo could tell Essa was brave, too.

"A pro tip, though, from one snoop to another. I've never been able to break into the top floor, where Frank and Victor have their private laboratory. No matter how many times I've tried, I can't get in. So don't bother. Or start there. Whichever, depending on how much you like a frustrating challenge!" Essa winked and then headed back downstairs for the kitchen.

Theo followed her, eyeing the servant staircase. The big main staircase stopped at the second floor, but they had seen windows for the third floor. In fact, this morning before the lightning strike, only a window on the third floor had been illuminated. So someone had been up there.

The servant stairs continued up past the second floor, but there was a sign politely stating that the top floor was off-limits. Which meant the top floor was exactly where Theo was most likely to find things someone didn't want found.

She crept up the stairs at exactly the same moment Essa reappeared in the kitchen.

"Where did you go?" Alexander asked. "Did the others need help?"

"No, it was nothing." Essa examined the cake batter and gave an approving nod. "Let's fizz it up!" They loaded the batter into the siphon—Alexander still half-afraid it was going to explode in their hands or shoot up into the ceiling like a rocket ship—and then sprayed the carbonated cake goo into a mug.

They both pressed their faces close to the microwave as it zapped the batter, watching it bubble up and up before settling back down as soon as the microwave dinged. They pulled the mug out, filling the kitchen with the soft, rich scent of chocolate.

"To science!" Essa said. "And to learning to bake things your mother can't!"

Alexander had raised the mug in a cheers before Essa finished, and then he felt guilty for cheers-ing something that seemed vaguely insulting toward his mother. He was sure she'd be able to make this if she tried. He would teach her how when they were back together.

"Sorry," Essa said, wrinkling her nose. "I get competitive when I care about things."

"So does Theo." Alexander softened again. Together, they scooped the funny, spongelike cake onto plates. Essa didn't touch hers, instead staring out the window at the moody ocean.

Alexander took a bite. It tasted almost right, but not quite. It looked and smelled like a cake he loved, but it was missing that special something that made it perfect. Maybe it was the lack of frosting, or maybe it was the strange airy texture. Or maybe what was missing wasn't an ingredient, but the person who always managed to make ingredients feel like more than just food.

Essa snapped in front of his face. "Hey!" she said. "No being sad on my watch! People don't like it when you're sad." Something about Essa's smile rang false, like artificial sweetener. No matter how hard sweeteners tried to mimic sugar, there was something that gave them away. An aftertaste that couldn't fool the tongue, that declared *I am not what I pretend to be.*

"That reminds me of our last camp." Alexander

frowned. "People should be able to feel what they need to feel. Have you ever been to Camp Creek by any chance? Met someone named Dr. Jay?"

Essa's face flickered with an unreadable emotion; then she tilted her head to the side. "I was at Camp Creek a few years ago. Didn't like it. But there was no one named Dr. Jay there when I went. Why?"

Before Alexander could explain, the door banged open to reveal a panicked Quincy. "Come quick!" She shot her lasso out and looped both Essa and Alexander. "It's an emergency!"

CHAPTER
TEN

Alexander had been afraid of an explosion in the kitchen. He *should* have been afraid of an explosion in whatever room Henry was in.

Henry stood in the center of the main science room, arms held out at his sides, covered in what could only be described as volcano vomit. If the rain had washed him enough to reveal his hair was dirty blond instead of mud brown, the volcano sludge had now dyed all of Henry an angry orange, which felt appropriate.

"What happened?" Essa asked.

"I got impatient." Henry glared, bracing himself with his hands in fists at his sides.

Alexander looked at Essa, waiting for her to shout or get mad.

Instead, she laughed. "You know what, sometimes you need to explode. I get it. And I probably should have supervised this one. But I have an idea for what we can do next. You want to break some stuff?"

Henry's goop-covered eyebrows rose. "I can . . . break things? Without getting in trouble?"

"Could I use my lasso?" Quincy asked as her dark eyes lit up and she tugged her cowgirl hat on tighter. "Could I use it to snag things and then tip them over and not feel bad if they break?"

"Oh, absolutely. We have a whole room for this. It's part of our mood and aggression unit. We call it the science of shattering. It's not all chaos, though. We test the strengths of different minerals, examine how glass shatters depending on how it was formed, and, my favorite, dip various food items in liquid nitrogen and then smash them with a sledgehammer."

Henry's eyes went big and googly. "I want to stay here forever," he whispered.

"Come on," Essa said, waving to Quincy and Alexander. "Let's go!"

"It sounds—" Alexander started. He wanted to stick

with Essa, to find out more about when she attended Camp Creek. Maybe she was connected to everything, after all, and just didn't know it. But he didn't want to go into the shattering room. It sounded dangerous. He didn't want his friends in a place where things were breaking and sharp pieces were flying everywhere.

As though anticipating his worries, Essa said, "We put on safety suits that cover all our skin, and also safety goggles, and also safety pins."

"Safety pins?" Alexander was confused.

Essa shrugged. "I like things to come in threes. The number three is very important to me. Safety pins was the only other *safety* thing I could think of. But I promise, I always put safety first. I'm not going to let *anything* happen to you."

She said it with such intensity, Alexander believed her. He was relieved to be with someone who prioritized safety. Essa was cautious, and it made him like her even more.

"I'll go find Dora," he said. "She won't want to miss this." Even though he knew they needed to be snooping, he also knew Theo would be upset to miss a chance to shatter a raisin with a sledgehammer. It was the only appropriate way to use a raisin, really. Plus, this way they could get Essa to tell them about her time at Camp Creek, and maybe get more information about Victor Stein.

Alexander found Theo stomping back down the servant stairs that led up to the third story. "Couldn't get in," she said. "How can I pick a lock on a door that doesn't have a lock?" She was in a terrible mood. The door to the third floor was massive, made of metal, and etched with a design that looked a little like lightning bolts. It also didn't have a doorknob, or a keyhole, or any means of opening it that she could find.

"I have a surprise for you." Alexander grabbed her hand and tugged her down the hallway to the main science room, where the others were already suiting up.

"We're going to . . . the moon?" Theo asked, looking at their extreme safety gear.

"No, that's later tonight," Essa said matter-of-factly. "Right now, we're shattering things. Smashing them to absolute bits and pieces, as hard as we want, as many times as we want."

"Yes." Theo nodded, eyes wide with awe and wonder. She was allowed to shatter things? Encouraged, even?

Alexander leaned close to her while Essa was distracted helping the others. "She went to Camp Creek a few years ago. She says Dr. Jay wasn't there then. We should ask her more about it, and also about Victor. You can get her chatting while you smash things."

"Right," Theo said, agreeing a little too fast. She was still mad that she had spent her time at Camp Creek being worried and pretending instead of actually having fun. At least here, she could combine sneakily gathering information with something that was genuinely entertaining.

Then she sighed. Alexander could gather that information without her. She had to focus on their priorities. "You work on Essa. I should go back to the campground and try to pick the book locks with my new aggressively borrowed tools." Theo watched the others finish preparing to smash the living daylights out of inanimate objects. She had never known just how much she wanted to do that until now.

"Absolutely not," Alexander said.

"Huh?" Theo asked.

"You can't go down to the campground by yourself. We all need to stick together."

"Alexander is right." They both startled, turning to see Wil. She had come back into the room, frowning as she scrolled through screen after screen on her phone, her eyes moving impossibly fast. "We have to stick together and each do our part. Unfortunately, Edgar and I aren't having any luck with internet research." Her voice was a low whisper so they wouldn't be overheard.

"There's no information on resummoning ghost aunts?" Alexander asked.

"Have you tried . . . Boo-gle?" Theo whispered.

Alexander let out a burst of a laugh, and Theo grinned, triumphant.

Wil rolled her eyes but couldn't hold back a smile. "The problem isn't that there's no information. The problem is that there's too much information, and none of it is reputable. Reputable means that something is respectable, that you could give a report on it and your teacher would give you an A because the report was so well researched and written. None of these sites are reputable. Everyone who wrote them watched too many scary movies and fake ghost documentaries."

"Oh, like *The Haunting at Haunted Hill*," Theo said. "I loved that one." Theo often watched ghost documentaries with their dad. He loved guessing what was actually happening behind the scenes. Toxic mold hallucinations was his most common suggestion.

Alexander shuddered. He hated the idea of breathing in mold even more than he hated the idea of hauntings.

"Let's not talk about ghosts while we're in a creepy old manor, okay?"

Wil put a comforting hand on his shoulder. "We *want* a ghost this time. It's different than being surprised by one."

"What about those boards?" Theo suggested. "The spooky ones where you put your hands on a thingy and it spells out words?"

Wil snorted. "Those were made by a game company. They're about as scary as Monopoly."

Alexander thought Monopoly was very scary. Being trapped for hours while Theo raged and schemed and got irate if he took a property she wanted? Terrifying. He had learned long ago not to play board games with her unless he was ready for torture.

"Besides," Wil continued, "Mom and Dad are the ones who summoned Aunt Saffronia in the first place, so they were only using things that could be found at our house. I'm trying to remember that night, figure out the details, but it's fuzzy."

"Candles," Alexander said.

"Candles," Theo agreed, shrugging.

"But Mom likes candles in general," Wil countered. "She always has a couple burning."

"True." Alexander racked his brain but couldn't think of anything else. It was all hazy.

Theo was thinking of other things. Namely, the classes at this science camp that were usually run by Victor Stein, who had known their mother. One class in particular was sticking in her mind now, thanks to their current conversation topic.

Essa was still helping Henry finish getting into his safety suit. It kept sticking on volcano goop, so it was a struggle. Theo waved Quincy over. Quincy had put her cowgirl hat back on over the top of the hardhat she was wearing, so that it teetered precariously.

"Hey," Theo said. "What about the undead class? Did you ask Essa about it yet?"

"Oh, that." Quincy waved dismissively. "It's focused on theories of reanimation, so I'm not interested. Besides, Essa said it's Victor's specialty. She doesn't have the lesson plan for it, or know much about it."

"Isn't reanimated the same thing as undead?"

Quincy laughed, a bold, bright sound, like she was lassoing her own happiness and flinging it around the room. "No, silly. Undead and reanimated are *totally* different things. Undead are things like vampires and zombies, fundamentally altered from their human form. And reanimated beings are brought back from death into their own bodies, or their slightly changed bodies. But still themselves. More or less. Y'all are so silly! Everyone knows that."

Alexander and Theo shared a puzzled look as Quincy bounced back over to help Essa finish suiting up Henry. Everyone definitely did *not* know the difference between undead and reanimated.

"Maybe it's a Texas thing," Alexander whispered. Who knew what went on deep in the heart of that infinite state?

"We really need Quincy to tell us more about her home," Theo agreed.

"But if Victor is an expert in things like reanimation," Wil said, tugging on one of her many long braids, "then he might have the information we need, even if Essa doesn't. Hey, Essa," she called. "Is there a library in the manor?"

Even in the middle of such an uncertain, sinister, upsetting summer, the unexpected answer Essa gave chilled all three Sinister-Winterbottoms to their cores.

"There is no library here," she said.

What kind of wretched place was this, anyway?

CHAPTER
ELEVEN

Alexander was grateful that the camp included three meals a day. And he was happy that he got to help make them, which meant that he hadn't had to go into the stressful shattering room. Quincy, Henry, and Theo were still buzzing, regaling the table with tales of shattering frozen food.

Quincy, in particular, had found great pleasure in destroying several of the foods she was allergic to. "Revenge!" she crowed, pumping a fist in the air. "Peanuts will fear *me* now!"

Theo was glad she had been able to forgive Quincy and that they were friends again. Even Henry had been fun to hang out with today. The shattering room was awesome, and afterward she had helped Quincy finish her volcano, which had also been awesome when it exploded as planned, unlike Henry's volcano.

But Theo couldn't quite relax. She hadn't been able to break into the top floor, and she couldn't try to pick the locks on the books until they were done for the day here. Essa had been so busy flitting from the kitchen to the various activities that it had been impossible to get her chatting about Victor or Camp Creek.

In fact, no one had accomplished their goals. Wil gave them a quick shake of her head as she sat down at the table. She didn't know yet how to resummon Aunt Saffronia. Edgar kept pushing food in front of her while she searched furiously on her phone for helpful information.

Mina joined them halfway through dinner, a firm grip on Lucy's hand. Lucy was covered in cobwebs and dust, and Mina's perpetually sweet face managed to look a little cross.

"Where was she?" Theo whispered. Essa was distracted at the other end of the kitchen, whipping something for dessert. The sound of the beaters covered their talking.

"In the vents," Mina answered, sighing. "I spent all day tracking her down and didn't even *see* Mr. Frank, much less talk with him."

"But you saw a lot of the manor?" Alexander asked.

"Every room that wasn't locked. This first floor has several themed science camp rooms in addition to the central room and the kitchen, plus a few guest rooms that aren't furnished yet. The second floor is also mostly unfinished guest rooms, plus the central science camp hub and a few themed camp rooms. There are stairs to the third floor, but the door there is locked—"

"Doesn't even have a handle," Theo grumbled.

"—and there are stairs to a basement or cellar, but that door is also locked. There's a second-floor room that's locked as well."

"So we have our targets for tomorrow." Theo smiled at Mina. "Thanks."

"Did you find anything, Lucy?" Alexander asked.

Lucy's big, dark eyes were wide as she held out her free hand, closed in a fist around something. Alexander and Theo leaned across the table, breaths held. At last, a discovery! Lucy opened her fingers to reveal—

A spider, carefully cradled so she wouldn't squash it.

Alexander jerked backward, nearly falling out of

his chair. He didn't kill spiders, but that didn't mean he wanted to hold one. After all, it was hard to identify dangerous spiders like brown recluses, so he assumed *all* spiders were brown recluses. Except daddy longlegs. For some reason, they never bothered him. Maybe because they were so awkward and goofy he felt sorry for them. They weren't even real spiders, which he knew because, as with most things Alexander was afraid of, he had done a tremendous amount of research on arachnids.

He found researching often helped him with his fears. So much of fear was rooted in the unknown. If he could understand, say, the average yearly number of spontaneous sinkholes and whether or not anyone had ever died in them, he was less likely to be consumed with a constant underlying dread that the ground would drop out from under him at any given moment.

Unfortunately, this didn't always work. On some level, Alexander knew that it was logistically impossible for an alligator to make its way up through narrow pipes and into a toilet, but his brain still refused to accept that reassurance. It also didn't work in the case of spiders. He knew most were harmless, but his brain took one look at those eight elegantly creepy legs and said ABSOLUTELY NOT.

Theo was also disappointed that Lucy held not a clue, but an arachnid. A spider certainly wasn't going to provide any answers as to how to find their parents. "Is that your sixth-favorite animal?" Theo asked, hopeful that this day might be good for something, at least.

Lucy shook her head, looking disappointed in Theo, as usual. Theo slumped in her chair, folding her arms crossly.

"Why did you bring back a spider?" Alexander asked.

Lucy spoke so softly it was difficult to hear her, her mouth barely opening. "To feed the frogs."

"What frogs?" Theo asked.

But Lucy had already lost interest in their conversation. The odd little girl used Mina's distracted soup sipping to slip beneath the table.

Wil moved to Lucy's now-vacant seat and leaned across the table like she was examining the variety of bread laid out. After lunch and between shattering sessions, Alexander and Essa had experimented with yeasted breads versus quick breads versus flat breads, and studied the history and effects of yeast. The results were delicious.

"Anything?" Wil asked.

"Nothing concrete. Essa went to Camp Creek a few years ago but didn't know Dr. Jay. We'll try to get more information about that, and about Victor."

"Yeah, nothing concrete here, either," Wil sighed.

"So you had a bad day?" Alexander asked, feeling guilty that, despite their lack of sleuthing success, he and Theo had actually had a lot of fun.

Wil glanced over at Edgar, sitting at the opposite end of the table. Their eyes met, and their mouths tugged up in mirror images of a small smile. Then Wil cleared her throat and leaned back in her chair, looking cool and composed once more. "I wouldn't say it was *bad*. But it wasn't productive."

"I like it here," Alexander said sadly. He enjoyed being here with his siblings and their friends. He liked the activities. And he really liked Essa. It was easy to be around her, like they had always known each other. Even her moods struck him as familiar—a temper and competitive spirit like Theo, occasional inexplicable distance like Wil, and worry about safety like him. "But if we don't find anything in the next day or two . . ."

"We should move on," Theo said reluctantly. She ripped the inside of her roll out, smashing it into a small ball in her hands. "There's still another family we haven't found yet."

"The Sirens," Wil said.

Alexander solemnly smeared some butter on his own

roll. "We could try to find them and get our answers there."

Wil also seemed disappointed with the idea. "Maybe we can come back here later this summer, with Mom and Dad." They were all quiet then, staring down at their dinners, hoping such a thing would be possible.

At last, the beater noise died. Essa rejoined them at the table, presenting a bowl brimming with fresh whipped cream to go along with the siphon cakes and sliced strawberries. "Better eat dessert quickly," she said.

"Why?" Quincy twirled her lasso in the air, ready to snag the bowl of whipped cream before Henry could grab it.

"Because," Essa said, and she smiled, looking straight at Alexander and Theo. "We need time, and we need to look closer."

Alexander's hand shot out and found Theo's. Essa had just said almost *exactly* what Aunt Saffronia told them before taking them to the water park and the spa, where they had found the timer and the magnifying glass.

Essa's smile didn't budge. "And," she said, "we need to stick together."

CHAPTER TWELVE

"What do you mean, we need more time?" Theo demanded, her hand going over her chest, where her timer was hiding. It was worn on an antique brass chain around her neck, and she kept it tucked under her shirt when she wasn't using it.

"What do you mean, we need to look closer?" Alexander held his breath, waiting for the answer. He also held his magnifying glass, safely stored in his jacket's large pockets. "And why do we need to stick together?"

Essa tilted her head quizzically. "I just meant we won't have much time to use the telescope to look closely at the moon. The sky won't be clear for long. And the rest of the evening is group activities, so we'll all be sticking together. Why? What did you think I meant?"

Alexander released his breath and shook his head. "Nothing," he said weakly. He barely had the heart to eat the siphon cake they made for dessert.

Theo definitely had the heart to eat it. "This was all delicious. And I'm entirely confident every food-safety protocol was followed."

Alexander nodded. "All of them. This kitchen is the best. It has everything I could possibly want, and Essa knows how to bake almost as many things as Mom. But with equipment to make things we can't make at home."

Theo shot to her feet, a look of absolute intensity on her face. Alexander didn't know what had occurred to her, but it had to be big. Maybe she figured out some crucial clue!

"Essa," Theo said, her heart in her throat. She shouldn't dare to hope, not after today's disappointments, not after what the rest of this summer had been like. But she still carried her dearest hope, always. She couldn't help it.

"Yes?" Essa's eyebrows lifted in concern at Theo's expression. Everyone around the table leaned closer.

"Do you have a deep fryer? *Can you make churros?*"

Alexander leaned back in his chair. Theo hadn't had a breakthrough about their most pressing concerns. Only about *her* most pressing concern. But he couldn't even be mad, because if anyone deserved churros, it was Theo. Especially after how hard she had worked to save everyone at Camp Creek.

"Does your mom make you churros?" Essa asked, tilting her head to the side. "Does she have a special recipe we can improve?"

"No, we've never made them at home before. But what is summer without a churro?"

"Didn't the chef make them for you at Fathoms of Fun?" Edgar asked, setting his teacup onto its delicate saucer.

"Yes, but that was ages ago!"

Alexander frowned. "That was, like, two weeks ago."

"Well, it feels like it's been months since Fathoms of Fun. Please, Essa? Tell me you can make churros."

Essa smiled like a cat with a bowl of cream. "*Absolutely* I can. I'll make sure we have everything we need for tomorrow." She hurried to the cupboards to find the deep fryer.

Theo threw one fist in the air in triumph, then sat back in her chair in relief, nodding at Alexander and Wil. "See, now even if we don't find what we need here, it hasn't all been a waste."

Wil snorted a laugh, reaching across the table and ruffling Theo's always-wild hair. "You have strange priorities."

A flash of guilt went across Theo's face. "But this isn't a priority. *Should* we focus on finding the Siren family instead of staying here another day or two?"

Alexander looked to Wil for the answer. It was nice having her actually notice them. Wil had told them she'd pay more attention, and she was really doing it. Wil glanced up from Rodrigo.

"Honestly? I don't think Mom and Dad meant for us to go on adventures. I think they sent us to Aunt Saffronia to keep us safe. Obviously, things have changed. This summer is going to be strange and scary no matter what until we figure everything out. But I think it's still good to find things to be excited about. To be happy about." She shot another look in Edgar's direction.

"Churros are my Edgar," Theo said.

Wil immediately glared at her, and Theo burst into giggles. Alexander couldn't help but join, and then Wil did, too, and then everyone at the table was talking and laughing and letting themselves be kids in the summer, if only for a few stolen hours.

The fun didn't stop there. Essa took them to a new room, where they climbed into a replica space shuttle. It was shiny metal painted with space symbols and had a door that opened up instead of out, like all futuristic, sciencey doors ought to. The shuttle was set up on top of hydraulic legs, which Essa explained used water pressure to move the shuttle around so it simulated flight without ever actually leaving this spot. She even let Alexander stay out of the shuttle and help her with the controls, because the idea of being in an enclosed space that was moving around—even knowing it was safe—made him nervous. After the space shuttle ride was done, Essa took them to the moon.

Or rather, she took them to the huge telescope on an ocean-view balcony where they could *look* at the moon. The telescope was ancient. It wasn't sleek plastic, but rather heavy, worn metal. Essa tinkered with it, adjusting various lenses and shifting the view, until at last she had it positioned correctly.

She was right—they didn't have much time. There was only enough clear sky for the moon to punch through for a few minutes. They each took turns looking at it as Essa told them about the phases of the moon, the way the moon affected Earth with its own gravitational pull and caused the tides, and how to create a tide chart to keep track of when the water was high or low.

"What's your favorite phase of the moon?" Theo

asked Essa as Henry bounced impatiently behind Wil, waiting for another turn at the telescope. Theo and Alexander kept trying to corner her so they could work the conversation back to Victor and Camp Creek.

"Everyone likes full moons," Essa said. "They shine the brightest and are the prettiest. No one likes new moons, when it's still there, but it's dark and you can only see it if you're looking right at it. I feel bad for new moons. I understand them."

Before Alexander could ask Essa more, disaster struck. Henry's impatient bouncing got too aggressive. He bumped into Wil, who stumbled and knocked over the telescope.

"That wasn't my fault!" Henry shouted, ready for them to get mad at him. When no one did, he slinked into a corner.

"I'm sorry." Wil crouched next to the telescope.

"I'm sure it's fine." Essa joined her. They righted the big, heavy instrument, moving it back into place.

"Oh no." Wil picked up a small piece of metal from the balcony floor. "This must have fallen off." She frowned at it, holding it up. "What part of the telescope did this belong on?" It looked like a key, with an ornate metal scroll on one end. But unlike a key, it had no prongs. It was a smooth length of metal where a key's jagged and pointy bits would be. Wil held it closer, narrowing her eyes. "That's weird."

"What?" Essa asked.

"It has my initials on it. Worked into this design. See? W.S."

Theo and Alexander looked at each other. Theo's hand went to her timer, and Alexander's hand went to his magnifying glass. Both of them had their initials, too. And both were objects Aunt Saffronia had wanted them to find when they went into Fathoms of Fun and the Sanguine Spa. Could this be connected? They needed to talk to Aunt Saffronia now more than ever!

"That is weird," Essa agreed. "Because wouldn't your initials be W.E.? For Willow Eurtton?"

Everyone froze. Theo, Alexander, and Wil shared a horrified look. They'd all been so focused on the object, they hadn't remembered their fake names.

"S is her middle initial," Theo blurted. "It stands for S . . . tupendous."

"Your middle name is Stupendous?" Essa raised one eyebrow.

"Yes, our parents wanted us to have something to live up to," Alexander said, hurrying to fill the awkward silence. "Willow Stupendous, Dora Sensational, and my middle name, is, uh—" He froze. All the s-words he could think of were filled with panic about how bad this lie was. Silly. Stupid. So-so-so-obviously-not-true.

"Superfluous!" Quincy chimed in.

"That's an awfully mean name for a twin." Essa frowned. "You do know it means not needed because everything that's needed is already there. It's not nice to feel superfluous. Not nice at all."

Quincy gave a high-pitched nervous laugh. "Did I say Superfluous? I meant—"

"Sensible," Alexander said with a rush of relief. "My middle name is Sensible."

"And he lives up to it!" Mina was holding Lucy's ankle as the little girl tried to scale the stone exterior of the manor, straight up the side of the balcony. "No one is more wonderfully sensible than our Xander."

"I can see that." Essa nodded thoughtfully.

"I guess I'll give this back, then, so we can fix the tele-scope," Wil said, holding out the strange smooth key. She looked at it like she usually looked at Rodrigo, and it was clear she didn't want to give it up.

Essa shrugged. "I don't think it belongs. Look, the metal on the telescope is silver, and that's brass. That key must have gotten stuck on the telescope when it was in storage or something. I pulled it out and fixed it up only yesterday. Besides, the telescope isn't broken." Essa gestured at it. Quincy stepped up to take her turn, flashing a nervous smile at Theo and Alexander to congratulate them on their barely covered-up mistake.

"So what should we do with this?" Wil's fingers curled gently over the key that wasn't a key. Alexander and Theo understood how she felt, because their objects had had the same effects on them. Like somehow, they had been meant to find them.

"Well, it's been in storage for at least twenty years, so no one needs it. And it has your initials on it, doesn't it, Willow Stupendous?" Essa laughed lightly, looking out over the ocean. "Clearly you were meant to have it. Think of it as a souvenir of our time together."

Wil nodded absently, tracing the edge of the key that wasn't a key. "Thanks."

When stormy clouds reclaimed the moon, their evening was done. Alexander and Theo hung back with Essa on the balcony as the others gathered their things before descending to the campsite once more.

"So, about Camp Creek," Alexander said. "When we went, it was . . . bad. Really bad. What was it like when you were there?"

Essa leaned on the stone balcony, staring out across the dark ocean. It was hard to read her expression without more light, but she sounded as far away as the moon behind the clouds. "It was fun, until it wasn't."

"What happened?" Theo asked.

"Remember that word? Superfluous?" Essa held up a pale hand as though she could catch the clouds and drag them down to earth. "I had some really good friends. Like you have here. But then they decided I was superfluous."

"That must have hurt," Alexander said. He'd had a good friend in first grade who decided Alexander was boring, and stopped playing with him. Even though they had been little kids at the time, it still made a special sort of aching pain flare up in Alexander's chest whenever he thought about how it felt to see his best friend turn his back on him and leave him behind.

"It does hurt," Essa agreed.

"But no one, say, took you into a tie-dye room and made things spin and convinced you that you liked everything good and normal?" Theo asked.

"And buffet-style eating?" Alexander added.

Essa laughed brightly, coming back from wherever her mind and memory had drifted to. "No, no tie-dye or spinning. And nothing was normal that summer. Nothing at all. Well! Good night. Come back in the morning first thing for breakfast. No reason to wait until the ten a.m. start time when we're all friends now."

Essa walked them down and stood at the back door waving, her white clothes the only source of brightness in the night. Still, they were all cheerful, knowing their next day would start with a great meal. It's easier to be happy in the dark if you know what the morning will bring.

As they all carefully navigated the cliff trail back down, Theo and Alexander filled the others in on what Essa had said about Camp Creek. "It doesn't sound like she was braindyed there," Theo finished, "so she must have attended before Dr. Jay took over."

"I don't remember her," Henry said. "But I didn't pay much attention to the campers when my dad was running the camp. They were mostly annoying."

"Tomorrow, get her talking about Victor," Wil said as they reached the bottom of the trail.

"Wait," Edgar hissed, holding up a hand. A cloud briefly parted for the moon, bathing the parking lot in cold white light. And revealing a large, hulking figure crouched next to their van.

CHAPTER
THIRTEEN

Before they could get a good look at the figure next to the van, clouds once again covered the moon, like someone had thrown a blanket over a lamp.

"Who's there?" Wil demanded. "If you mess with us, I'll hack your phone, steal your identity, and ruin your credit scores."

"*And* email all your friends a confession that you still pick your nose!" Theo added.

No one answered.

"What should we do?" Alexander whispered. He was sensibly worried. Sensible really would have been an excellent middle name for him.

"There's eight of us and one of them." Theo cracked her knuckles. "We have numbers on our side."

"Seven of us," Henry said.

"What?" Alexander turned and then covered his mouth in horror. "Where's Lucy?"

Mina looked down at her side, where Lucy no longer was. "Oh no!" Mina gasped. "Someone will get hurt!"

"I'm sure Lucy will be fine," Theo said, hoping it was true.

"It's not Lucy I'm worried about." Mina rushed forward into the parking lot. They all ran alongside her to the van. They found no sign of the hulking figure, which was a relief. As big a relief as what they did find: Lucy, sitting on top of the vehicle, kicking her heels against the side of it.

"Lucy Blood!" Mina put her hands on her hips. "You get down here right now. What have we said about approaching menacing strangers?"

Lucy scowled, her lower lip jutting poutily.

"It's good to learn about stranger danger," Alexander cautioned. Their parents always said it was important not to move through the world in fear, but it was also important to be aware and alert.

"Yes, she can be very dangerous to strangers," Mina

agreed with a sigh, even though that was definitely not what Alexander had been referring to.

"Should we keep looking?" Quincy asked, twirling her lasso through the air and scanning the parking lot in case someone was still lurking about.

"No. If someone was here, they're gone now. And nothing seems to be disturbed. Maybe it was just someone using the restrooms." Wil's face was illuminated by Rodrigo's blue glow. She didn't look like she believed herself, but with no sign of the lurking figure, there wasn't much they could do. Edgar unlocked the van, and Henry dragged the camping gear out of it.

"I'm the only person who knows how to set these tents up," the boy said. "So I get first pick!"

"Thank you, Henry." Alexander patted him on the shoulder. "You've helped a lot. We're glad you're with us."

"Well, you *should* be glad I'm with you!" Henry shouted.

"I . . . am? That's what I said."

"Oh, right." Henry let out a long breath. He wrapped his arms around himself, the way Theo had showed him. "Sorry," he grumbled. "Once my aunt took over at Camp Creek, everyone was mean to me. No one was ever glad to see me. It was easier to get mad at them before they had a chance to make me feel bad." He paused, thinking. "I'm going to try to stop doing that to you all. But also to be nicer to myself, too. It's okay if I'm angry sometimes, as long as I'm not mean."

"Anger is a perfectly normal reaction," Edgar said. "A feeling like other feelings: happiness, sadness, excitement, butterflies every time your fingers brush someone else's." He studiously did not look at Wil when he said that part, and Wil did not look at him, but Theo was pretty sure they were both trying their hardest not to split their faces apart with giant smiles. She didn't think she'd ever be that silly even when she was a teenager.

Edgar cleared his throat and continued. "There's no reason to try not to feel anger. But I think you're smart to express it and feel it in ways that are less, um—"

"Aggressive?" Alexander offered.

"Explosive?" Theo suggested.

"Combative?" Quincy contributed.

"Aggressively explosively combatively emotive," Alexander settled on.

Theo went to ruffle Henry's hair, but it was still goopy from his volcanic eruption, so she settled for patting him on the shoulder. "And while you're figuring it out, we'll be here. We're your friends."

"You're stuck with us." Quincy snagged him with the lasso as though to prove her point.

Henry's voice was tight as he nodded and said, "Okay. I'll try to remember that. Now let's set up some tents before I get too tired. I turn into a monster when I'm tired."

There were three tents in total, along with several sleeping bags and a couple of camping lanterns. Henry and Edgar took one tent; Lucy, Mina, and Quincy took another; and the Sinister-Winterbottoms took the third. Wil immediately crashed into sleep, Rodrigo pressed against her cheek like a pillow.

By the cold light of the camping lantern, Theo began working on the locks. Alexander sat next to her, yawning, his eyes drifting shut. They hadn't gotten any sleep the night before, and he was as tired as he could ever remember being. But he didn't want Theo to feel lonely being the only one awake while everyone else was asleep.

"I'm good at picking locks," she muttered, fiddling with the Sinister book lock. She switched from the tiny screwdriver to one of the lengths of wire. The hammer taunted her, but she worried if she smashed the locks, the books would get damaged. "I don't know what I'm doing wrong. If only the key Wil got wasn't toothless and useless. Maybe that could help."

"You'll get it. I know you will." Alexander yawned again, which made Theo yawn, which made Alexander yawn even bigger. They laughed over infecting each other with the yawns; then Theo set the books aside and lay down with a huff.

"I'm going to close my eyes for a minute before I get back to work," she said.

"Mm-hmm," Alexander agreed, lying next to her. "Just for a minute."

One minute later, they opened their eyes to the dim gray light of morning.

"Drat," Theo muttered, throwing an arm over her eyes. "That was a very long minute."

Alexander sat up, blearily blinking as he ran his fingers through his hair to comb it neatly down. Theo's hair surrounded her head like a halo, if the halo belonged to an angel that had recently been electrocuted. She didn't finger-comb it, because she didn't care. They were both chilly and sore from sleeping on the hard ground all night. They also had no idea if it was too early to go up to the manor yet.

"Wil," Alexander said, nudging her.

"I'll destroy you," Wil groaned, burrowing deeper into her sleeping bag.

"Maybe I can get some more lock time in before every-one wakes up," Theo said. "What if I brought one or two up to the house to work on?"

Alexander understood why she wanted to, but he didn't think it was a good idea. Not when they knew Edgaren't was looking for the books. "Mr. Frank hardly seems trustworthy. We'd probably better keep them locked up and hidden in the van."

"What about one?" Theo asked. "I could bring the Stein book up. It would make sense for it to be in the house. No one would look at it twice."

"Unless they knew what they were looking at." Alexander was torn, though. Theo was right. This was a huge priority. And she couldn't stay down here by herself to work on the books. It wasn't safe to be alone, and besides, they had no food. "My jacket pockets are big enough for books," he said, which was true. He was a very practical boy and always chose jackets with pockets big enough to tote a book around. You never knew when you might need emergency reading material. He passed his jacket to Theo.

She gave him a grateful smile. "Thanks. I'll be careful with the book. And your jacket."

"I know you will." And Alexander meant it. Maybe at

the beginning of the summer he wouldn't have trusted Theo to be careful with something so important. After all, she had a long history of leaving things in odd places. Homework in the fridge. Shoes in the bathtub. Her retainer every place imaginable, including, inexplicably, the time Alexander found it being used as a bookmark. But he knew Theo knew how important these books were. And that she'd take care of his jacket, knowing he liked to keep his things nice.

"When do you think we should go up?" Theo stood and stretched, her hair going even wilder with static as it brushed the top of the tent.

Alexander unzipped the tent flap and peered out. Then he rubbed his eyes and peered out even harder. "What the what?" he whispered, staring at the pathway up the cliff.

The pathway that had been clear last night was now completely blocked by enormous boulders. Someone didn't want them returning to the manor.

CHAPTER
FOURTEEN

"It had to be Frank!" Henry raged, stomping around the tumble of enormous boulders blocking the cliff path entrance.

"Maybe they fell during the night?" Mina offered as she buttoned her vest. With the exception of Lucy, who was staying safely shaded in the tent until it was time to go, the others had joined them in various states of readiness. The Sinister-Winterbottoms, Quincy, and the Bloods had their luggage with them, but Edgar and Henry didn't, and the campsite restrooms didn't have showers. Henry was as disheveled as ever, his hair still mostly orange and his shirt and shorts a color that defied understanding but looked like something you'd put down the garbage disposal. Edgar appeared as though he had been up for hours, his black hair perfectly styled, his three-piece suit remarkably unwrinkled. Quincy was redoing her two long braids. She looked unfinished without her cowgirl hat atop her head.

Theo was good at understanding how her body moved through space and good at understanding how other things moved, too. She pointed up the sea cliff. "Look. There aren't any break marks from where boulders would have fallen, and there are no gouges on the cliffs from sliding rocks. With boulders this big, we'd see their pathway if they had fallen down. And we also would have heard them in the night. It would have been super loud."

"But who could have silently moved them here?" Alexander asked.

"Who do we know who's huge and hulking and always lurking about, telling us to get lost?" Theo asked.

"Mr. Frank." Quincy glared at the rocks. She had already tried lassoing them and tugging, but they didn't budge. Even pushing together, the kids would be lucky to shift any of the boulders. And because of the steep ascent of the cliffs, they couldn't go around. There was no way for them to get to the path from down here.

"We shouldn't assume that it was Mr. Frank." Mina was wringing her hands, looking at the rocks. "But what do we do now?"

"I'll bet I could climb around them. Or scramble over the top of them." Theo was already looking for the best hand- and footholds.

"I'm sure you could," Wil said, "but that doesn't mean the rest of us can." She looked exhausted. Her braids were coiled into a bun on top of her head, and she was only scrolling half-heartedly through websites on summoning ghosts.

"Oh. Right." Theo deflated, kicking at one of the small stupid rocks in front of the big stupid rocks. "I guess we walk up the normal road, then."

"I can't risk Lucy being in the sun that much," Mina fretted. The gray clouds were wispy, threatening to let the sun break through at any moment.

Edgar tucked a purple handkerchief into his suit pocket, letting the corner stick out to provide a pop of color. "If we take the van and park it in front of the manor," he said, "anyone looking for us will be able to see it from the road. They'll know exactly where we are. The campground isn't part of the manor, so at least down here the van is hidden."

"It's low tide." Theo gestured to where the restless gray waves were farther down the beach than normal. "Which means we can walk along the shore and look for the other path up. Alexander and I saw one that led to sea caves, so I'll bet it starts down here."

While the ocean had ebbed to its lowest point, it still left only a narrow strip of rocky beach between the dark, hungry water and the dark, brutal cliffs. "But low tide turns into high tide," Alexander said. "And if we don't find a way up, we might get caught by the water on the beach." He couldn't stop imagining being pinned between the waves and the rocks, the water rushing forward with nowhere for them to run. He liked looking at the ocean, but he had no desire to touch it, much less be swallowed by it.

"I think we can make it." Theo really wanted to catch a glimpse of the sea caves and see what was so off-limits about them.

"But what about when we need to come back down?" Alexander asked. "We don't know what the tide will be like then. Risking discovery feels safer to me than risking the ocean. We've been discovered before, and we always make it out by running away or tricking Edgaren't. We can't do either of those to the ocean."

Theo looked like she wanted to argue, like she wanted to tell Alexander to be just a little braver. And, truth be told, she did want to do both of those things. She was confident they could find another path up before the tide turned. At worst, their shoes might get a little wet.

But she remembered forcing Alexander to go down a water slide at Fathoms of Fun without taking the proper precautions, and how poorly it had turned out. And she remembered accidentally forcing him to break the rules at the Sanguine Spa, and how it had caused a fight between them that hurt them both. And she remembered how desperately she had wanted her own cautious Alexander back when Camp Creek had changed him.

Theo sighed and turned away from the ocean. "Okay. Van it is."

"Who put you two twerps in charge?" Wil asked. But it was clear she didn't mean it, and that everyone else trusted their judgment, too. Alexander felt a warm burst of pride that they all trusted him, followed by a cold rush of fear that he was going to let them down.

Theo felt a prickly burst of annoyance that she wouldn't get to climb a giant jumble of boulders or search for a sea cave pathway, followed by a sticky rush of begrudging acknowledgment that Alexander had made the right choice—she had one of the family books in her pocket, and she couldn't risk letting it get wet. Not after she had promised Alexander she would take care of it.

They took down the tents, loaded the van, and climbed in. The vehicle groaned and bounced up the narrow, serpentine campsite road that eventually spat them out onto the main road. Edgar pulled into the gravel circle in front of the manor entrance, trying his best to tuck the van into the sparse, wind-bent trees so it was less visible from the road.

Without a word, Henry hopped out and began grabbing handfuls of mud from yesterday's leftover puddles. Before any of them could ask what he was doing, the first gob of mud slapped against the side of the van. Then another, and another.

At first, Theo thought Henry was having a temper tantrum. Then she laughed. "Camouflage!" Sure enough, by the time they had all climbed out—on the side of the van that wasn't being pelted by mud pies—the view from the road would show a van absolutely covered in muck, with no visible identification.

"There," Henry said, chest heaving, hands dripping in sludge. "That was a trick I learned hiding under the cabins at Camp Creek. The muddier I was, the better I blended in."

"I'd give you a high five," Alexander said, "but . . ."

Henry actually smiled. "We can wait until after I wash my hands."

With Lucy once again swathed in a poncho so no stray beams of sunlight could land on her, they all marched up to the front door. Alexander much preferred this door, because there was a whole manor between them and the edge of the cliff now. The front door was even bigger than the back door, soaring overhead and curved at the top like an archway. Stained-glass windows on either side of the door had a zigzag pattern that made the glass look like bolts of electricity shooting out.

Quincy rang the bell. Once again, it tolled from somewhere inside the manor, a bone-rattling sound.

The door swung open, and Frank looked down at them, deep-set eyes widening in surprise. He looked almost green with shock, fingers gripping the edge of the door. "You can't be here—" he started, his voice a tortured creak. He took a step forward, enormous hands outstretched to grab them.

CHAPTER

FIFTEEN

All the kids and teens scurried backward, but before Frank could reach any of them, a bright voice chimed behind him.

"Here you are!" The door opened the rest of the way to reveal Essa. "Why did you come to the front door today, instead of using the back entrance?"

Theo wrinkled her nose at Frank. "*Somehow*, the path up here got blocked by a bunch of large boulders only someone very strong could move."

"That's odd!" Essa smiled at Frank. "It's a good thing we have Frank here. Be a dear and go clear it."

He glared at her, his expression flat and menacing, much like the top of his head.

"Go clear the path," she said again, her voice still bright like the sunlit ocean, but with an undercurrent of something flashing, finned and toothy, in the depths.

With a complaining groan, Frank lumbered away.

"I'm so glad you're all here!" Essa said, not explaining Frank's behavior or what had happened to the path. "Breakfast is ready, and we have such a day ahead of us! Tide pools and circuitry and slime making and the most unbelievably scary but still perfectly safe demonstration of the laws of physics using a bowling ball suspended from the ceiling and swinging right at your face!"

"That sounds like a perfect day," Quincy said, her eyes big with awe.

Essa nodded, more sincere than excited. "I've worked really hard to make sure everyone knows they have a place at *my* camp. That you're all wanted and valued." Her face did that thing where it went far away and almost gray, like a storm over the sea.

"No one is superfluous," Alexander said gently.

Essa blinked, and then her smile was back in place. "Exactly. It's going to be the best day."

They ate breakfast (after Henry washed his hands and then dunked his head under the kitchen faucet for good measure, too, lightening his hair to a now even sandier blond) while Essa finished setting up the various stations. Essa had actually made toad-in-the-hole after Alexander mentioned it yesterday, and it *was* delightful, all buttery and flaky and sausagey.

Theo talked around a mouthful. "I guess sometimes when the British give weird names to things they're actually good. As opposed to, say, traditional mincemeat pie."

Mid-bite, Wil slapped her forehead. "Mincemeat pie! Fathoms of Fun! Charlotte!"

"Blue whales! Pineapple soda! Torches!" Quincy shouted.

"Huh?" Wil asked.

"I thought we were just shouting random things." Quincy shrugged.

"No, I was thinking aloud." Wil turned to Edgar. "Let's call Charlotte and ask her how to summon Aunt Saffronia again! She should know!"

Charlotte was one of seven nearly identical sisters who helpfully haunted Fathoms of Fun. Alexander didn't like to think about it. Not because Charlotte was a ghost— which was upsetting in general—but because it meant that most of their time at the water park they hadn't had registered, certified lifeguards watching out for them. Charlotte had been very kind and helpful, but could a ghost perform CPR? Would a ghost even understand what CPR was?

Alexander shook his head, trying to shake himself out of worrying. Sometimes he got snagged on something scary or stressful or embarrassing that had already happened and he couldn't stop his brain from gnawing on it, like a dog with a terrible bone made out of anxiety.

Edgar grimaced. "That's not possible."

"Why?" Theo asked. "Can't she talk on the phone? Aunt Saffronia could."

Edgar glumly stirred his tea. "Charlotte can talk on the phone, but there are no phones at the water park anymore."

"What happened?" Alexander asked. "Did Edgaren't come back? Did they cut the phone lines? Is it sabotage by Mrs. Widow's evil sister?"

"No, no," Edgar said, holding up a hand. "Nothing like that. Phones didn't go with the overall theme of the park. My aunt felt like they clashed with the aesthetic."

"What's an aesthetic?" Henry demanded.

"It's a fancy word for style." Edgar was an expert on

aesthetic. Whether wearing an old-timey striped bathing suit and holding a parasol, or sitting at a table at science camp wearing a three-piece suit with a flower tucked into his top button hole, he always looked exactly like he wanted to. "Unfortunately, in this case," he continued, "my aunt's style demanded that there not be any phones."

"That seems like a safety issue," Alexander said.

"Not really." Theo gestured at Wil. "After all, everyone *else* has phones these days. If there's an emergency, any guest in the park can call for help."

Wil set Rodrigo on the table as though putting the phone in time-out, even though it wasn't Rodrigo's fault that Charlotte couldn't be called. "But *we* can't call any guest in the park, because we don't know anyone there right now. Is there any other way to contact someone at Fathoms of Fun? There's no email address listed on their website, which looks like it was drawn by hand a hundred years ago."

"Telegram," Edgar said, ticking ideas off on his long fingers. "Messenger pigeon. Morse code transmitter."

"Did you want to do a class on Morse code?" Essa swept back into the kitchen. Today she wore a pink sundress, practically glowing in contrast to the dull gray rock of the manor. Her light brown hair wasn't in a ponytail, instead rippling down to the middle of her back. Everything about her was bright and young and pretty. She didn't look like she belonged in Stein Manor at all, where everything was gray and heavy and looming.

"You have a Morse code transmitter?" Wil asked. She and Edgar stood in unison.

"I think so. I pulled a lot of weird things out of storage in the basement. Let's go find it! The rest of you, a slime station is set up in the main science room. You can get started, and then we'll test how different varieties of slime react to things like water, acids, and glitter."

"Glitter," Henry whispered, his eyes widening.

"Acids," Quincy whispered, her eyes widening.

"Safety precautions," Alexander muttered, his eyes narrowing. After yesterday's volcano accident, he wasn't comfortable letting Henry anywhere near acid. Or glitter, for that matter, which was almost as bad.

As Wil and Edgar followed Essa out, the others looked to Theo and Alexander for what to do next. Well, except for Lucy, who had already disappeared. Mina sighed and stood. "Back to work, then. I'll try to find Mr. Frank, too, and speak with him if I can." She left in a swish of skirts.

"I'm going to crack this lock." Theo patted the pocket of Alexander's borrowed jacket where the Stein book was safely tucked away. "Alexander, you're with me?" Alexander nodded, and Theo turned to Quincy and Henry. "Keep Essa busy, you two. And pump her for information on Victor."

"And maybe don't use the acid for anything," Alexander added.

Quincy saluted, using her lasso to snag a bottle of syrup from the counter and drown her poor toads in all their holes. "You can count on us."

"We know we can," Alexander said with a smile. "We should have come up with a cool team name."

"Team You Can't Make Me?" Henry suggested.

"Team Yee-Haw!" Quincy said.

"Team Sneak," Theo said.

"Team SOS—Save Our Summer," Alexander said, Morse code still on his mind.

"That's the one," Henry said with a scowl. "I'm mad I didn't come up with it."

"Well, let's get a move on." Quincy lassoed the kitchen door and held it open for them all with one booted foot. Theo always wore sneakers so she could run and climb, but she very much liked Quincy's brown cowgirl boots with their patterns of flowers, birds, and what looked oddly like hands reaching up from the grave.

Theo and Alexander parted ways with Quincy and Henry on the second floor as the other two headed for the slime-making stations with a vow to leave all acid handling to Essa. The main science room was on the far side of the manor, past all the other rooms and across the fancy open stairway from the entrance room with the big fireplace. That staircase had rails made out of dark metal formed to look like lightning bolts, a theme in the house.

Theo frowned back at the servant stairway that was the only way up to the third floor, which had only one door. The door she hadn't been able to get through. Neither had Essa, for that matter.

It bothered her almost as much as not being able to guess Lucy's sixth-favorite animal. When Theo was fixated on something she wanted to get done, not finishing it felt like an itch in the middle of her back she couldn't reach. Or, more appropriately, like when someone shouts, "You have a bee on your back!" but no matter how many times you whirl around, of course you can't see your own back. And even after the person assures you the bee has flown away, you're not entirely sure it really is gone. For all you know, there could be a bee on your back right now.

Theo whirled once, trying to see whether that itch in the center of her back was the restroom bee, having hitched a ride to freedom, but then shook her head. She had to focus. No fixating on bees outside or inside her body, and no stewing over the un-unlockable door on the third floor. She had a different lock to work on. "Let's find somewhere quiet and hidden so we don't get disturbed."

"Mina said this floor was all science rooms, plus a few unfinished guest rooms and one locked room. We could use one of the empty guest rooms." Alexander gestured to the doors lining the hallway. The carpet was deep green, and the doors matched that shade. They were bolted to the walls with big black metal pieces that looked sturdier than necessary.

Theo tried door after door down the hall until she found the one that wouldn't open. It was the last room before the fancy stairs that sat in the middle of the house. Unlike the door on the third floor, this one had a heavy black doorknob, complete with a keyhole gaping open like an invitation. Theo pressed her eye to the keyhole, but she couldn't see any details of the room beyond. "There's probably a reason it's locked, right?"

"Yes. To keep us out."

Theo grinned. "True. But also, if it's locked, no one

will think to look for us in there. After all, what kind of twelve-year-old is good at picking locks?"

Alexander sighed but gave Theo a reluctant grin. "Only the you kind of twelve-year-old."

"Exactly. Only the me kind of twelve-year-old, and Mr. Frank doesn't know that." Theo pulled out her tools and got to work. Fortunately, the tiny screwdriver was a perfect fit, and after reshaping one of the thin metal wires to wrap around it, Theo needed less than a minute before the latch clicked and the door swung slowly open.

"It's an office." Alexander was mildly disappointed but also relieved that it wasn't something more interesting and therefore scarier. A huge window framed the sullen ocean like a painting. In front of it lurked an imposing, dark wood desk. The walls were lined with bookshelves bursting with books. And on every possible surface, there were papers and notebooks and piled-up drawings. A long leather couch was the only thing not covered in work. The cushions were sunken deeply in on the side closest to the desk, like a very large person regularly sat there.

"But whose office is it?" Theo asked. If it was Mr. Frank's, then it wasn't a great idea for them to hang out here.

Alexander stepped carefully in, tiptoeing over the deep green rug that took up the center of the room. On the desk, swimming in a sea of paper, notebooks, and worn-down pencils, was a framed picture. Two men stood in front of the ocean, arms around each other's shoulders, captured mid-laugh. It was the happiness that made Alexander take a moment to recognize who the taller man was.

"That's Mr. Frank," he said. He couldn't imagine Mr. Frank smiling, but now that he saw photographic proof, he knew the dour man had a wonderful smile.

"That must be Victor, then." Theo peered down at the photo. They had seen a picture of V. Stein as a teenager, but it was hard to remember exactly what he looked like. Theo picked up the frame to get a better look, but her hand slipped. The frame skittered off the desk, shattering on the floor.

"Be careful!" Alexander said.

"I know. This isn't the shattering room, after all." Theo bent down, mindful of the broken glass. The frame itself was broken, too, one of the corners jarred apart. It revealed something as unexpected as Mr. Frank's smile. Theo carefully pried out the photo and unfolded the section that had been bent behind the frame, unseen. Lurking in the corner of the hidden portion of the picture, watching both Frank and Stein, was none other than . . .

"Mrs. Widow?" Alexander gasped.

"No." Theo pointed to her eyes, which weren't covered by Edgar's unusual purple glasses. They weren't the eyes of the real Mrs. Widow.

They were the eyes of her evil sister.

CHAPTER
SIXTEEN

"The fake Mrs. Widow!" Theo and Alexander said at the same time.

"They know her!" Alexander couldn't believe it. Here they had been expecting signs of Edgaren't, and instead found fake Mrs. Widow, right there in a photo.

"Didn't the real Mrs. Widow say something about a Frank, when she was talking about all the bad things her sister had done?"

"I think she did! So this proves it, then. Mr. Frank is bad. He's working with the fake Mrs. Widow, who works with Edgaren't. Mr. Frank must have done something with Victor Stein. That's why Victor's not here, and why Essa doesn't know when he'll be back. We were exactly right to suspect him."

"It wasn't hard. He even looks suspicious." Theo stuck her tongue out at the photo.

Though, in the photo, Mr. Frank looked different. Younger. Happier. Tanner. In comparison to back then, now he looked half-dead. Alexander supposed that was what happened when you chose to be mean.

"You search the desk," Alexander said. "I'll concentrate on the bookshelves. Maybe we can find information about Victor, or where he is."

"We have yet to find a secret passage in the manor. Maybe we'll luck out and there will be a detailed map." Theo sat down at the desk and began pulling open drawers. There were, in fact, a lot of detailed drawings, but none of them were maps. They were anatomical, drawings of veins and tendons, hearts and lungs. Page after page of them, with cramped, scrawled notes crawling all over the empty spaces. "I think Victor Stein is a doctor."

"Really? I was about to say I think he's an electrician." Alexander was reading spine after spine of book titles about electricity, electrical currents, and the use of electricity to regenerate and reinnervate human tissue. He knew *regenerate* meant "to generate again," meaning "to create or grow again," but he had no idea what *reinnervate* meant. Maybe something with nerves. He was definitely feeling some nerves right now, since they were hanging out in a place run by someone in league with Edgaren't. Again.

"Remember when lightning struck the manor?" Theo frowned at diagrams that looked like an operating table wired to a dozen cords. Like their charging center at home, where there were always too many cords plugged in. Only in this case, the cords would connect to . . . a person? It didn't make any sense.

"And the whole place lit up after. Maybe they use lightning power as energy? Is that even possible?"

Theo shrugged. "People use solar power and wind power. Lightning power doesn't seem safe, but if they have a steady supply here and know how to capture it, then maybe. Wil *has* been commenting on how fast her phone charges plugged in here."

Alexander was still looking at book spines, less and less convinced he would find anything useful. They were all textbooks and nonfiction about electricity or medical things. "Speaking of capture, we'd better hurry so we can tell the others what we've discovered about fake Mrs. Widow and Mr. Frank." He pulled out one book without a label on the spine. It was a thin leather folio, filled with loose papers. Opening it, the first thing he saw was an official document. A document that made absolutely no sense. "Theo," Alexander said, his heart racing.

"I'm almost finished going through the drawers, and then—"

They had been so busy talking to each other they hadn't heard sounds they definitely needed to be listening for. The sound of a key turning in a lock, and then the sound of a door swinging open, and then the sound of two enormous, booted feet stepping into the office.

"You can't be here." Frank's voice was a low rumble, like distant thunder warning that a storm was coming. His sunken eyes were glaring at them, their pale, filmy color unnerving beneath his heavy brow.

Alexander squeaked, slamming the leather folder shut. He had to tell Theo what he'd seen in there. It felt like his chest would burst from trying to hold it in. "Sorry, we, uh, we thought this room was okay to use. For research. For the camp."

Frank took another step into the office, filling the entire doorway and blocking their way out. "You can't be here," he said again, the rumble of thunder voice getting ever closer and louder.

"Why?" Theo stood, hands on her hips. They knew

who he was now, so odds were good he knew who they were. She didn't see any reason to pretend otherwise. "Because you're worried we'll discover your secrets?"

"I have no secrets," he whispered, but it sounded tortured.

"Oh, really?" Theo held up the de-framed photo. "Then how do you explain *her*? We know who she is, what she does!" Theo jabbed a finger at the fake Mrs. Widow.

To Alexander's surprise, Mr. Frank didn't look angry, or sneaky, or cruel. He looked . . . stricken. The blood drained from his already sickly face, and he put a hand over his heart, his impossibly broad shoulders turning inward like he was in pain. "Please," he whispered. "Please listen to me."

Theo rolled her eyes. "So you can tell us we can't be here again? Get a new line. We're not going to listen to anything you say."

Frank closed his eyes and then took a deep breath. His voice, when it came out, was as terrifying as lightning striking the manor had been. "Take your friends and get out!" He rushed toward them.

Theo ducked under his arms and ran out of the office, Alexander hot on her heels. She slammed the door behind them, taking the tiny screwdriver and hitting it into the lock with the tiny hammer so it was all jammed in. They raced through the hallway, down the servant stairs, and into the empty kitchen. It was the place Alexander felt safest. Leaning against the counters, they sank down to the floor, out of breath, hearts still pounding.

"So that proves it, once and for all. Mr. Frank is bad."

"There's something weirder, Theo." Alexander tried hard to catch his breath. "In a folder, the one I found right before he came in . . . there was a death certificate. A death certificate for *Mr. Frank*."

"What?" Theo couldn't believe it.

Neither could Alexander. "I didn't get a chance to look at the dates or the signatures. But it was definitely a death certificate, and it was definitely for Mr. Frank."

"Wait, wait. Are you saying he's a ghost?"

"No! He doesn't remind me of Aunt Saffronia or Charlotte at all. And besides, we already know Edgaren't's gang are more than happy to imperson-ate other people. Remember in that photo? Mr. Frank looked like a different person than he does now. I think *this* Mr. Frank isn't the real Mr. Frank. I think he's an imposter, because the real Mr. Frank died. And now that Victor Stein is mysteriously gone, and no one here knew the real Mr. Frank from before, this imposter stepped in to take over."

"Classic." Theo nodded in admiration. She had to give it to Edgaren't and his crew. They were good. "So Mr. Frank isn't Mr. Frank. But he doesn't know we know, so we have to keep pretending."

"Something is confusing me, though," Alexander said.

"Only one thing?" Theo laughed. "Because a lot of things have confused me lately."

Alexander nudged her with his shoulder. "The thing most currently confusing me is that the Count tried to keep us at the Sanguine Spa for Edgaren't to come get us. Same with Dr. Jay. She tried to keep us at Camp Creek."

"Yeah," Theo agreed, wondering where Alexander was going with this.

"But the fake Mrs. Widow tried to drive us out of the park, because she didn't want us to find Mr. Widow and stop her from destroying Fathoms of Fun to get to the oil underneath it."

"Right."

"So what changed? What made Edgaren't decide to try to grab us rather than making us leave?"

Theo pulled out her timer. She nodded to the pocket

where Alexander kept his magnifying glass. "We found these. And the books. He wants them."

Alexander nodded. "But if fake Mr. Frank—"

"Mr. Fake," Theo corrected. "No relation to the Ekafs."

"Yes, Mr. Fake is working with Edgaren't, shouldn't he want us to stay until Edgaren't can get here and claim us? Steal the books back, and take our things?"

"He—" Theo frowned. "Yeah, actually. But every time we've been alone with him, he's told us to leave."

Alexander didn't want to say what he was going to say next. He wanted to go and get the others, climb into the van, and escape before anything bad or scary happened. And he knew if he told everyone that was the best plan, they would listen to him. Because they trusted him.

Once again he felt that sick pit of fear, that terrible worry that their trust in him was going to get them all in trouble. But he was good at thinking through situations from all angles, at analyzing them, at imagining every possible scenario. That was what his brain did. And his brain was telling him two things, very clearly.

"One," Alexander said with a sigh, "if Mr. Fake wants us to leave, that means there's something here he doesn't want us to discover. It must be important if he's so desperate to get rid of us. And two, last time we thought we were chasing Edgaren't to Camp Creek, but he was already one step ahead of us. He used Dr. Jay to keep us there. This time, we know exactly what and who we're dealing with. We won't get tricked."

"So we can be ready," Theo said, realization dawning on her. She smiled a terrible smile, a devious and wonderful smile. "This time, when Edgaren't shows up, *we'll* be the ones who trap *him*."

CHAPTER
SEVENTEEN

"Wait, wait," Wil said, slipping Rodrigo into her pocket. That was when Alexander and Theo knew things were serious. She tugged a few braids free of her bun and ran them through her fingers, like she did when she was deep in thought. "So we know that the real Mr. Frank is dead, and this Mr. Frank—"

"Mr. Fake," Theo corrected.

"Right, Mr. Fake is connected to the fake Mrs. Widow, and therefore to Edgaren't, and that means we're going to . . . stay here?"

"It makes sense to me," Quincy said.

Then her friendly face went a little worried. She fussed with her cowgirl hat, pulling it on lower and tighter as though it could hide her. "But I don't really want to see my uncle again."

They were sitting around the table in the kitchen, lunch finished. It had taken until lunchtime for them all to be together again. After their confrontation with Mr. Frank, Alexander and Theo had rejoined Henry and Quincy, figuring there was safety in numbers, but Wil and Edgar hadn't shown up again until now. Lucy was still nowhere to be seen, but Mina was here, wandering around the kitchen, opening every cupboard and even several of the drawers hoping to find her.

"We had no luck reaching Charlotte," Edgar said with a frown as elegant as a pinkie raised while he took a sip of tea. Theo liked Edgar, and people were always saying he had good taste, but she knew tea didn't taste good, so it didn't make sense to her. "And you four had no luck getting details about Victor Stein."

"Yet," Alexander said hopefully. "Every time we brought him up, Mr. Fake interrupted the science class and Essa had to shoo him out, or Henry accidentally spilled acid, or some other near disaster."

"Thank goodness I never spilled the glitter," Henry said. No one had the heart to tell him that his hair was now sandy blond with remnants of orange goo highlighted with so much glitter it looked like a unicorn had vomited on him.

"I sort of talked with Mr. Frank—Mr. Fake—there are lots of code names," Mina said, sitting at the table with an exhausted sigh. "Anyway, I found him coming up from the basement. I introduced myself and told him I'd love to help him by looking over their plans for the bed-and-breakfast and giving any feedback I could think of. He grabbed my wrist and started pulling me down the hallway with some urgency, when we were interrupted by Essa, who told him it was time to go clear the path and she didn't want to see him again until it was finished."

"Where do you think he was taking you?" Alexander said with a shudder, hating the idea of Mina being in trouble without anyone knowing.

Mina patted his hand, which made him feel like he was going to throw up. It was very difficult, having a crush on someone. "Don't worry. Lucy would never let anything happen to me. Just like I don't let anything happen to her."

"How would she know, though?" Quincy asked, gesturing to the thin air around them.

"Listen," Theo interrupted. "Before Essa gets back, we have to finish our plan. It'll work."

Wil's expression was dubious. "I know you're confident, but—"

"I think it will work, too," Alexander said.

Edgar adjusted the lovely green silk tie he was wearing. He didn't have luggage with him, but he did have pockets full of accessories to change depending on his mood. "So your plan is that we explore the manor and look for places to lure Edgaren't—calling him that still makes me feel silly—into a trap, all while avoiding Mr. Fake, who wants us gone."

Theo nodded. "We know what Edgaren't wants: the books."

"It seemed to me he wanted more than the books." Wil was idly toying with the strange toothless key she had found.

"Well, whatever he wants, he'll come here for it. We trap him, and then he has to give us all the answers we need." Theo was certain of it, bouncing in her seat with excitement.

"He told us he didn't know where our parents are," Alexander said, troubled.

"He's a liar." Theo waved dismissively.

Alexander agreed that Edgaren't was a liar, but in this case, he believed that Edgaren't really didn't know where their parents were. Which was part of why he thought they should stay here. If there were answers in this manor, they needed to find them. *First.*

"So, in the meantime," Theo said, "you all spend the afternoon looking for anywhere we could trap Edgaren't. There has to be somewhere. A secret library, or passages, or even a sturdy broom closet. I'll keep working on picking this book's lock. I know I can do it." She patted the jacket pocket where the book was waiting for her. "And Alexander is going to keep Essa busy so she doesn't get in anyone's way. And everyone will watch out for Mr. Fake. But don't let him know we're onto him."

"I should keep researching how to resummon Aunt Saffronia," Wil said. "You've changed our priorities."

"To more pressing priorities!" Theo insisted. "Besides, you can explore and use your phone at the same time. You do it a lot."

Wil let out an annoyed huff. Edgar nudged her with his elbow. "I'll keep you from wandering off any cliffs or falling into any pits. Promise."

Wil's huff turned into a small smile as she pulled out Rodrigo once more and got back to work. "Fine."

They all scattered, so that when Essa returned to the kitchen, it was only Alexander and Theo waiting for her. "Where is everyone?" Essa asked.

"Independent study projects." Theo hopped up to sit on one of the counters. She kicked her heels off the cupboard below her, bouncing them in a staccato pattern. "I'm going to use the mechanical engineering table all afternoon. I'll be very focused on my project. Do you have an activity you could do with Xander so he doesn't get bored?"

Alexander resented the fact that he had to play the part of the kid who would get bored if someone didn't give him something to do. He was almost never bored. He liked having long stretches of quiet time with nothing to do and no expectations so he could get appropriately lost in a book.

"Maybe something in the same room as Dora so she's not alone?" Alexander was worried Essa would suggest more kitchen experiments—which he actually loved, but he didn't want anyone alone and vulnerable to Mr. Fake. Though he supposed Lucy was technically alone wherever she was, and Mina was alone searching for her. But remembering how Mina had warned Lucy not to hurt a mysterious hulking figure in the night made Alexander suspect the Blood sisters were more than capable of handling things on their own.

Still, he wouldn't have minded if Mina joined him.

No, he thought, blushing. He would get all nervous and clumsy, and it would be humiliating. Better to have

Mina somewhere nearby and unseen than somewhere close by and very seen.

"I was going to do a class on tides and tide pools," Essa said. She seemed disappointed by the lack of kids in the kitchen.

"I don't want to go in the ocean!" Alexander blurted out. For a boy who was deeply afraid of many, many things, including but not limited to mushrooms, crosswalks, buffets, toilet alligators, wave pools, and causing his entire class to be punished for something when he hadn't done anything wrong, it was shocking that Alexander never listed sharks as one of his worst fears. But that was only because he could live his life in such a way that he was 100 percent guaranteed never to meet a shark on its own turf. If he never went in the ocean, he would never encounter those rows and rows of teeth and brutally elegant fins cutting like knives through the water toward him.

If he was forced to go in the ocean, he would definitely have to move sharks to the very top of his long list of terrible fears.

Essa shook her head. "We were going to go on a field trip to the beach tomorrow, not today. Today we'll learn about tides, how to read tidal charts, what affects tides, what can change them, and the ways they interact with beaches. Tides are fascinating. They're a liminal space—the thin line between one world and another, where ocean becomes land. And tidal pools are the tiny little puddles that exist in the middle of those liminal spaces. Improbable, delicate, fraught. Overlooked by most people, like so many liminal things are. Superfluous, when compared to the vastness of the ocean." Essa stared into the distance, her expression going cold and sad, like a tide pool just out of reach of the waves, slowly drying and bringing death to everything inside.

"I do want to see the tidal pools," Alexander said softly. "As long as I don't have to go in the water."

Essa's face shifted, once again sunny to match her cheerful dress. "Of course! I can't wait to show you. But that's for tomorrow, when we have everyone back together. Come on! Tidal charts and the science of the ocean wait for no one! Or for everyone, since they're eternal and endless."

Alexander and Theo followed Essa upstairs to the main science room. Theo took up a spot at the mechanical engineering table, surrounding her real work with big pieces of metal and engine parts so that, if Essa glanced over, she wouldn't be able to see that what Theo was actually tinkering with was a tiny lock on a book.

She was getting close; she knew it. It was maddening how long it was taking, but she was going to open this book, no matter what.

Alexander and Essa worked at a table overlooking the back windows with a clear view of the awesome vastness of the sea. Alexander didn't have to pretend to be interested in what Essa was showing him. It really was fascinating, and he was sad the others couldn't join them in learning about the tides and the way they affected ocean life and shorelines.

"You can tell the high-tide point along this stretch of the ocean by where these end," Essa said, holding a scattering of what looked like sharp pebbles in her hand. Alexander pulled out his magnifying glass to look closer.

"Oh," Essa said, letting out a breath.

Alexander froze. He never should have showed her the magnifying glass. He didn't even think about it.

Essa blinked rapidly as she smiled down at the pretty antique thing. "That's beautiful," she said. "What a good idea. I should have one of those for future classes." She held her hand out to give him better access to the pebbles.

Too late to hide the magnifying glass, Alexander leaned down and used it. The pebbles weren't pebbles at all, but some kind of sharp shell.

"These ones are dead," Essa said. "Dried out and lifeless. And the ones at the tide mark will look the same when they're dry. But when the waves come . . ." She moved her hands together, then opened them like a flower blooming. "Voilà! Life again. Tomorrow we can learn about symbiotic ocean life, where two creatures exist in perfect harmony. And what happens when they're separated." Her gaze drifted out over the ocean, the gray of the sky and the rock and the water reflected in her eyes.

"How well do you know Victor Stein?" Alexander said, unable to dance around it anymore.

"Not well. Not as well as I thought I did, at least." She frowned down at her tidal charts. "Who disappears when someone needs them?"

Alexander frowned, too. Their parents had. But he was sure they had a good reason, or that they hadn't disappeared of their own free will. "But is he a nice person? Not like Mr. Frank?"

"What's happened with Mr. Frank?"

Alexander backtracked. He didn't want to put Essa in any sort of danger. "Oh, nothing specific. He's just unfriendly. And he doesn't seem trustworthy, or like he wants us here."

"Oh, no, he definitely doesn't want you here. You

know, I think he's been trying to sabotage this camp from the beginning! Isn't that funny?"

"Yeah," Alexander said slowly. "Funny."

"But you let me worry about that old grouch. You should all avoid him. Like I said, if he tries to talk to you, come get me immediately and I'll sort him right out. He really wanted the bed-and-breakfast, I guess, so he wants the science camp to stop. And without Victor here, he's free to try and keep the science classes from working. That's my theory, at least."

"Yeah. Good theory." It was a good theory. Alexander wished he could tell Essa the better one. He changed the subject instead. "So, how does the moon affect the tides?"

By the time the sun had set and everyone had gathered around the table for dinner, Alexander's brain was filled to the high-water mark with information about tides and beaches and tidal pools, but still shallow with information about Victor Stein.

Theo, too, was frustrated and grumbling into her pizza. How was a lock on a book this difficult to pick?

"Hey, is there a basement, Essa?" Quincy asked, lassoing a shaker of Parmesan cheese. Even though she was mildly allergic to cheese, she felt the best topping for cheese was more cheese. "I found stairs going down, but the door at the bottom was locked."

"Oh, yes. It's small, and used for storage."

"*Storage*," Theo said, italicizing the word with her voice to make it sound like she was poking Alexander in the side. In their summer experience, storage was never storage. It usually contained a secret library, or tunnels, or a Widow locked away from her own park and husband.

Alexander nodded, and Theo nodded, and Quincy nodded, and Henry bit grouchily into his slice of pizza, piled high with red pepper flakes. "What a fun afternoon," he muttered. "No explosions, no shattering, just wandering around looking for—"

"Mold!" Quincy interjected. "For our project. We wanted to expose mold to different environments and see where it grew best."

Alexander's stomach turned, no longer in the mood for pizza now that mold was the topic of discussion. "Who made dinner?" he asked, looking quizzically at Mina. She'd been in here when they finished their classes.

Mina shook her head and then sighed at the empty chair beside her. "Not me. Too busy looking for Lu—uh, loose Susy."

Theo paused with a slice halfway to her mouth. If it was Mr. Fake's cooking, she definitely didn't trust it.

"I did," Essa said.

"How?" Alexander asked. "You were with me all afternoon."

Essa wiggled her fingers through the air. "Magic!"

"The magic of delivery?" Wil asked.

"The magic of preset oven timers?" Edgar suggested.

Essa laughed, still doing her wiggly fingers.

As though summoned by the gesture, a panel in the ceiling opened and Lucy tumbled through the air, landing right in the middle of the table and right on top of one of the pizzas. Unlike Henry, who seemed to get dirty with the slightest actions, Lucy stood up without so much as a grease stain on her flowing white frock. She left little footprints in the cheese as she primly stepped across the table, though.

"I don't like that topping," Henry said with a scowl.

"Where have you been?" Mina demanded.

Lucy held out both hands, which were cupped together, holding something. Alexander preemptively scooted back, anticipating another spider. But no one could have guessed what Lucy was holding as she moved her top hand away to reveal it.

CHAPTER EIGHTEEN

"Is that a *frog?*" Alexander asked, still wary. In Lucy's hands, even a frog seemed like it could turn into something scary.

Quincy leaned close. "It is! I don't know if I'm allergic to frogs. Can I test it?" She held out her hand, and Lucy gently passed it over. "Weird," Quincy said.

"Are you allergic?" Henry asked.

"No, not that. I mean, yes, I'm already getting hives. But what's weird is this." She pointed at the frog. In addition to the usual froggy spots along its skin, it had straight lines that were slightly raised, like scars. "I can feel them along its belly, too." Quincy gave the frog back to Lucy. Sure enough, Quincy's hands were now covered in red welts. "Guess I can cross frog wrangling off potential lasso-based careers."

"Those look like surgical scars," Edgar said, peering closer at the amphibian. "How did a frog get those?"

The frog blinked, offering no answers. Which was probably for the best, because a talking frog would leap right over a ghost aunt in terms of bizarre events, and Alexander had had enough of those for one summer.

"Where did you find it?" Wil asked.

Lucy pointed straight up.

"It was in the vents?" Mina asked.

Lucy once again gestured, pointing straight up.

Mina shrugged at the rest of them. "If she doesn't want to tell us, she's not going to. She's always been like this with her collections."

Alexander had seen one of Lucy's collections, a little nest inside the secret passages of the Sanguine Spa. It had been lovingly, creepily stuffed with clothes and blankets and papers and books and keys. Including the set of little keys that opened the family books. The ones that Edgaren't had taken away from them. Alexander really hoped Theo would be able to crack those locks soon. But he knew she was getting frustrated, so he didn't say anything.

Theo leaned close to the silent, big-eyed, frog-catching little girl. "Listen, Lucy." Theo glanced at Essa and cleared her throat. "Susy. This is *very* important. Is that frog your sixth-favorite animal?"

Lucy gave Theo a sad, disappointed look. She didn't even bother shaking her head no. Theo slapped the table with an exasperated groan. "I'm never going to get it!"

"Do you think they were experimenting on the frog?" Alexander asked, troubled. The frog seemed perfectly content—and perfectly healthy. It hopped out of Lucy's hand, landed in the salad none of the kids had touched because who eats salad when pizza is right there, jumped to the breadsticks, then leaped off the table and along the floor. Lucy waved goodbye, and before anyone could think to grab it, the frog disappeared under the door.

"It wasn't part of any science camp classes, was it?" Theo asked, looking at Essa.

Essa shook her head. "Goodness, no. I'd never harm a living thing. No matter what harm those living things might do."

"What harm would a frog do?" Alexander asked.

Essa blinked, coming back from wherever she retreated to when she was thinking. "Well, trigger an allergic reaction in poor Lacey, for one."

Quincy sighed. "I have allergy medicine in my suitcase in the van."

Thunder rumbled in the distance, and they all looked out the window. The evening sky was quickly turning to a stormy sky.

Wil stood up. "We should go. We have to set up the tents before it starts raining."

"Won't your parents do that for you?" Essa asked innocently.

Wil froze, glancing at the others. "They're, uh, very lazy."

"So lazy," Edgar said.

"The laziest!" Henry shouted. "It makes me furious!"

"Plus, they don't know how," Mina said, much more generously.

"They're gone," Lucy whispered.

Essa tilted her head to the side. "What?"

Theo glared at Lucy, but Lucy wasn't paying attention to her. "They . . . checked into a hotel for the night. But there weren't enough rooms for us, so we're all still camping. Because we love camping."

"We love it so much," Alexander said with a mournful sigh, thinking about the cold, hard ground, another night spent in a sleeping bag, another predawn wakeup stiff and sore and still tired.

"Well, be careful and stay dry out there. I'll see you all in the morning." Essa smiled, her reflection in the window a bright spot against the darkening night. She was still standing in the kitchen window as they climbed into the van outside. With a final wave, she melted from view.

"We've definitely told Essa too much," Wil said.

Alexander racked his brains. "Have we used our real names around her?"

Theo's face twisted in thought. "I accidentally called Lucy by her real name, but I corrected it. Maybe Essa didn't notice."

"She feels trustworthy, though," Quincy said. "Right? And she keeps helping us when Mr. Fake gets in our way."

Alexander nodded. Essa was more like one of them than an adult. "Still. We don't want to put Essa in harm's way by getting her mixed up in all of this. She should be free to have a summer of running fun science classes. We need to be more careful." He stared out the van window at the manor, which seemed to stare right back. Literally, in the case of the window on the third floor, where a distinctively large silhouette loomed, watching them leave.

Edgar pulled out of the parking area and drove them down to the campsite. It was already gusty, and pitching the tents was a nightmare. With the first drops of cold rain pelting them, they abandoned the two smaller tents and opted to all stay in the one large tent. But even a large tent wasn't large when filled with eight bodies.

"Now I know how a Vienna sausage feels," Theo muttered, crammed next to Alexander, who was crammed next to Wil, who was crammed next to Edgar, who was crammed next to Quincy, who was crammed next to Mina, who was crammed next to Henry. Lucy, somehow, was lying diagonally, taking up the most room of anyone in the tent despite being the smallest person in it.

Theo wanted to keep working on her lock, but there wasn't enough space. Everything was elbows and knees and bonking heads. The ground felt harder than it had the night before, when they were too tired to notice all the rocks bruising and poking and harassing them from beneath the thin layers of tarp and tent and sleeping bag. Wind clawed at the tent, tearing something loose on the outside that slapped and flapped against the canvas with far more noise than a simple strap should make. Before long, heavier rain began pelting down. The tent was waterproof, but the din was terrible.

"We're never going to sleep," Theo grumbled. She debated escaping into the van to work on the book lock in there. But she didn't want to go outside in this storm.

"I need to—" Henry started, but Wil cut him off.

"Don't say it!" she snapped. "Because if you say it, everyone else will need to, too, and I don't want us running through this storm to the—"

"Bathroom?" Lucy whispered, and everyone groaned.

Lightning flashed. Alexander began counting. But before he could even get to three, thunder crashed, the only thing louder than the rain and the wind. Lightning flashed again. He counted—he could hear Edgar and Quincy and Mina all counting under their breath at the same time. They barely hit two before thunder rumbled the air around them.

"It's getting closer," Alexander said, panicking. "Is this tent the highest thing on the beach? The restroom building is higher, right? So if lightning struck, it would strike the restrooms. Right? Are there any trees? I can't remember." He was breathing fast, unable to calm himself. There was too much noise, too much chaos. He wondered what would happen to a tent hit by lightning. He'd never researched that before, which felt like a huge failure on his part. He'd let himself down, and his family down, and his friends down, and they were going to be struck by lightning and it would be his fault for not knowing how a canvas tent would handle it.

"Maybe we should move to the van!" Wil shouted as lightning once again lit up the night so brightly it was like they had switched a flip to daytime. They were plunged back into darkness almost instantly, followed by thunder so loud they slapped their hands over their ears.

Henry sat up. "Water's coming in!" Sure enough, the rain was cascading down the sloped ground toward the ocean, and running right into the seam of the tent where it wasn't waterproof.

"What do we do?" Quincy said, grabbing her cowgirl hat and putting it on her head where it would stay dry . . . for now.

Light pierced their tent once more. But it wasn't from a flash of lightning. Someone was outside, shining a flashlight right on them. Mina grabbed Lucy, Quincy already had her rope coiled and ready, Henry's fists were balled up, Wil put an arm in front of Edgar to protect him, and Theo reached for Alexander.

The twins held each other's hands as tightly as they were holding their breath.

They'd been found.

CHAPTER NINETEEN

"Hello?" a voice called over the terrible tumult of the storm. The voice did not belong to a man with small, mean eyes and a large, mean mustache. Nor did the voice belong to a lumbering groaning menace of a manor owner.

The tent flap unzipped, revealing Essa. Her smile glowed like a lighthouse in a tempest. "I worried about you in this storm, with your parents at a hotel! Come spend the night in the manor. Get your things together, and I'll meet you back up there!" She waved and hurried away.

No one needed convincing. They scrambled out of the tent, zipping it up and leaving it to the night rather than trying to wrestle it back down. Everyone piled into the van and tried not to be scared as Edgar steered. Water poured down the road into the campsite, so it was like driving upriver. Lightning flashed all around them, with thunder so loud they couldn't talk.

By the time they reached the manor, all the first-floor lights were on. This time the windows didn't feel like eyes watching them, but like beacons guiding them to safety. Henry's mud camouflage had washed clean off the van, but it felt genuinely dangerous to stay out tonight. They could deal with it in the morning.

"Bring in the luggage," Wil said. "Everyone can share the dry clothes." After two days, Edgar and Henry were ready for a change of clothes, even if it meant the clothes didn't fit them well.

Well, maybe Edgar wasn't quite ready. He looked sad as he glanced down at his once-impeccable suit, now rumpled and half-soaked.

"What about the books?" Theo asked.

Wil looked torn, then nodded. "Yeah, put them in Alexander's suitcase. That way we'll have them with us, where we know they're safe and we can get them if we need to."

Alexander and Theo moved some of his clothes into her bag so that they could fit the books in his. Suitcases in hand, they raced up the walkway to the entrance, barely able to see through the storm.

"What if Mr. Fake opens the door and won't let us in?" Alexander shouted.

"What?" Theo shouted back. "I can't hear you! I'm worried Mr. Fake is going to open the door and not let us in!"

Fortunately for everyone, Essa opened the door before they even had a chance to knock or ring the doorbell. "Come in!" she said. "Take off your wet shoes. I'll get them dry and back to you." Everyone did as they were told.

Essa was somehow already dry, her light brown hair in a bouncy ponytail, her pink sundress exchanged for a pale blue nightgown, her feet bare as always. "I've always wanted to host a slumber party!" She laughed her silvery laugh. It was a welcome sound after the terrible clash and roar of the storm outside. In the manor, they could still hear the tempest, but with so much solid stone around them, they felt safe.

Well, almost all of them felt safe. Alexander meekly raised his hand. "We saw lightning hit the manor the morning we got here. What happens if it hits it again?"

Essa guided him into the sitting room. A fire roared in the fireplace, and the couches had been pushed back. Pillows lined the floor, along with enough blankets for everyone to make a nest. Though the space was still cavernous and intimidating, with the gray stone floors, gray stone walls, and lack of warmth, Essa had done her best.

"Don't worry about lightning," she said. "Victor rigged something to the top of the manor that channels it. Powers the whole place, actually."

"Explains the charging," Wil said, plugging her charger into the wall and letting out a happy sigh, watching Rodrigo guzzle up the electricity.

"I wondered if that was how it worked!" Alexander exclaimed. "If he has a system to use the lightning, then it won't hurt us. Right?"

"I'm not going to let anything hurt you." Essa bent over so they were eye level, locking her hazel eyes onto Alexander's brown eyes. "Okay?"

"Okay." He nodded. He believed her. Not just because he wanted to, but because he had been lied to a lot this summer, and he was getting better at knowing when people were telling the truth.

She clapped her hands, straightening. "Since none of the guest rooms are finished, I thought it would be most fun for everyone to sleep down here together!"

Alexander was a little torn. Their family had a no-sleepovers rule. But this wasn't a sleepover; it was a slumber party. And it was with his sisters and their friends. And he felt safer with everyone together, especially since Mr. Fake was still around here somewhere.

Theo wasn't torn at all. She wanted to jump into a pile of pillows, to burrow in, to stay up late telling scary stories and eating too much ice cream. She knew she should work on picking the Stein book's lock, since she still had that one in her pocket, but it was late and they were all a weird combination of exhausted and alert, thanks to the storm.

"Why don't you all take turns in the bathroom off the lobby? Hot showers will be just the thing for you all. I'll get some cookies in the oven for us!" Essa practically skipped away. If they were relieved to be inside, Essa was thrilled to have them there.

"She loves having us around," Alexander said.

"Why wouldn't she? We're delightful," Theo answered.

"I think she's sad and lonely. I see it sometimes."

"Really? I was going to say I think she's brave and also a little angry."

"We need to talk," Wil declared.

Everyone paused what they were doing and turned toward Wil. She stood in front of the great stone fireplace, her back to the flames. Her face was serious, Rodrigo charging on the floor instead of held under her nose. "We don't know when Victor Stein will be back, or even if he's coming back. Whatever there is to find in the manor, we haven't found it yet. And between Lucy, Theo, and the rest of us, we've been over almost every inch of it."

"Where *is* Lucy?" Mina muttered, looking around. "How does she always do this?"

Alexander pointed straight up. Lucy had somehow managed to climb the walls to where the stone fireplace chimney met the ceiling. She was perched there on a tiny ledge of rock, watching them, her eyes reflecting the lights so they seemed to glow in the dark up there.

"Anyway," Wil said, "we haven't found anything worth finding. And we know that Mr. Fake isn't on our side, which means we're at risk here."

"But—" Theo started.

Wil held up a hand. "We gave your plan a shot, twerp. It was a good idea. But I can't keep everyone here, knowing at some point Edgaren't will come for us. There hasn't been a response to our Morse code transmission, so in the morning we'll go to Fathoms of Fun. We can get answers from Charlotte about how to find Aunt Saffronia again. And Edgar's real aunt and uncle might be able to direct us to wherever the Siren family is, since the Stein family was a bust."

"No!" Theo stomped her foot. "We know there's something here worth discovering. Otherwise, Mr. Fake wouldn't be trying to get us to leave. And we know Edgaren't will come for us here, which means we can be prepared for once."

Wil shook her head. "It's up to me to keep you safe. All of you." She looked around the room at sweet Mina, terrifying Lucy, plucky Quincy, angry Henry, and even calm Edgar. "It's time to move on."

Theo let out an exasperated growl. Wil was wrong. She knew Wil was wrong. Theo turned to Alexander for support, but Alexander looked unsure. Wil's plan was the more cautious one, so of course he would choose it. Theo didn't know how to argue, or even if she should. Maybe she was being stubborn. But she hadn't accomplished anything here that she set out to, and it was driving her bananas. She *hated* losing.

Her bees were frenzied in her chest, demanding action, buzzing and filling her with so much noise and agitation that she didn't want to say anything. She was worried it would all come out like stingers, angry and mean and not helpful to anyone.

"I'm going to take a shower," she grumbled, grabbing a change of clothes out of her suitcase. Her hand went around her timer. She'd have to take it off to shower, but with everything falling apart around her, she knew something terrible would happen. It would fall off the sink and shatter, or get lost down a drain, or be gobbled up by a rogue toilet alligator.

Scowling, she took the timer off and handed it to Alexander. "Hold on to this for me while I shower. I'll probably break it or something, since obviously I can't be trusted."

Alexander accepted the timer, looking down at it sadly. "I trust you."

"I know," Theo huffed. It came out sounding crosser than she meant it to. "I learned how to be cautious. I wish everyone else could learn to be a little braver." Theo stomped off toward the bathroom, trying to ignore her chest full of bees demanding she abandon being reckful and do something, anything, genuinely brave and heroic and reckless.

Alexander watched her go and wished he could be a little braver like she needed him to be. Wil's plan was the more cautious one, but like in the tunnels underneath Camp Creek when he wanted to go a different direction, Alexander couldn't shake the feeling that they weren't making the right choice.

CHAPTER
TWENTY

After her shower, Theo was too mad to go back into the main room with everyone else and pretend like she was still happy to have a fun slumber party. Instead, wet hair dripping on her shoulders and feet bare against the chilly stone floors, Theo wrapped herself up in Alexander's jacket and followed her nose to the kitchen. Essa was humming as she twirled around, dozens of cookies cooling on the counters. When had she found the time?

Theo slumped into one of the chairs around the large table.

Essa stopped dancing. "What's wrong?"

"My sister decided we're all leaving in the morning."

"You can't!" Essa's voice cut through the air with the same percussive power as a burst of thunder. Her hands were clenched and raised as though she were searching for something to do with them, some way to release the emotion that had risen like a tsunami inside her.

"I don't want to," Theo said, feeling defensive in the face of Essa's surprisingly emotional outburst.

Essa looked wildly around the kitchen. Finally, she grabbed a plate, dumped a bunch of cookies on it, and slammed it down in front of Theo. "Tell me those are better than your mom's."

Theo poked at the plate. She didn't even feel like eating cookies, which was evidence of just how rotten she felt about this decision. "We shouldn't go."

"I agree you shouldn't. We still have so much to do. At the camp, I mean." Essa sat across from Theo, smoothing down her hair in an attempt to calm herself. "Besides," Essa said, her voice softer, "I've loved having you here. Getting to know you."

Still mad at Wil, Theo made a snap decision. It didn't matter anyway, if they were leaving. "We didn't come here for science camp," Theo said. "Even though that part was

actually fun, and you did a great job. We came here looking for answers."

"What kind of answers?" Essa picked up one of the
cookies and slowly reduced it to crumbs as she broke off
piece after piece.

"About our families. Our parents aren't here at all.
Which you probably guessed when they never, ever
showed up, and we said they checked into a hotel without
us, leaving us in a storm."

Essa shrugged. "I figured something was up, and that
you'd all tell me if you felt like I needed to know. Everyone
has secrets. Where are your parents, if they're not here?"

"They're missing, or gone."

"You don't know where?"

"No. It's a mystery. That's why we're here. They all
knew each other when they were younger, and they knew
Victor Stein, too. Something happened back then, at
Camp Creek. We think it might be tied to why they're
missing now."

"What makes you think that?"

Theo let out a frustrated huff of air. "Because those
are the only clues we have. All we know is at the beginning of the summer, everything was normal, and then
one night, without warning, all our parents left. And now

we're running around, having the weirdest vacations ever, trying to find them before anyone else does. There's a man with small, mean eyes and a large, mean mustache, and a bunch of other bad people, as well, including Mr. Frank, who isn't even Mr. Frank. He's Mr. Fake."

"Not Mr. Ekaf?" Essa's eyes twinkled. "Perhaps he's related to the Eurttons, unless that's *not true*, either."

Theo slouched guiltily. "You figured that out, huh."

"I wondered why you were playing a trick on me. But it wasn't on me at all, was it? It was on Mr. Frank and these other 'bad' people looking for you." Essa brushed the remains of the demolished cookie off her fingers. Her hazel eyes were practically electric, crackling and sparking with intensity. "If you're looking for answers, then there's something I need to show you."

"Really?" Theo's heart skipped, her bees buzzing wildly as though preparing themselves. "I'll get the others, and—"

"No," Essa said. "We have to go right now, quietly, so we don't alert Frank to what we're doing. I *knew* he was being weird about all of you. So many things make sense now."

"He's not even the worst of them. But yes! Let's go!" Theo half wanted to insist they at least bring Alexander, but if Essa said they needed to go right now, then they would. Essa led her down the servant stairs. At the bottom was the locked basement door none of them had gotten through yet. Essa looked over her shoulder at Theo, winked, and turned the doorknob.

It wasn't locked anymore. The door opened to reveal a cramped and crammed basement filled with old furniture, paintings, appliances, what looked like operating tables—or maybe long, narrow metal kitchen tables—wire coils, engines, and all sorts of electrical gear. If Theo could fly over it all and see it cut into sections, the basement would be on the front of the manor by the entrance, and the section at the back of the manor against the edge of the cliff wasn't dug out at all.

"What is this?" Theo asked.

"Storage," Essa answered.

"It's never just storage," Theo said, confident.

"No, it really is just storage." Essa shrugged. "Nothing worthwhile in here. But it does lead us to . . ." Essa pushed aside an old moldering mattress—*moldering* being a word for disintegrating that also sounded like moldy, which was appropriate here because it was also moldy. Theo was glad Alexander wasn't here. He'd already be thinking of ten terrible things that could happen by coming into contact with mold growing on an old mattress in a damp basement. And if this were an episode of *The World's Most Haunted Hauntings*, her dad would be crowing in triumph, pointing to the screen and saying, "Mold hallucinations!"

But this wasn't a haunting, it was a mystery. And Theo couldn't even worry about the mold, because the mattress moved aside to reveal . . . the entrance to a tunnel. That must be why the basement didn't extend farther. Theo rolled her eyes. "Would you believe before this summer I never once encountered a secret tunnel but lately I can't seem to avoid them?"

Essa laughed. The sound echoed like wind chimes through the darkness ahead of them. "I would, in fact, believe that. I've been through many a secret tunnel in my time, and they all have one thing in common."

"What?"

Essa beckoned Theo forward. "Answers."

Casting one last glance behind herself, wishing Alexander was with her to remind her how brave she was, Theo followed. The tunnel twisted and turned, dropping steeply. It was damp and cold inside, the air itself wet. "Are these the sea caves that the sign warned everyone away from?" Theo asked.

"There's a whole network in this cliff. The tunnels all flood, up to a certain point. Very dangerous if you don't know where you're going." Essa walked confidently through the darkness. There were no lights down here. All Theo could see was the pale blue glow of Essa's swishy nightgown leading her forward. A few times Theo caught herself from tripping on the uneven tunnel floor, saved only by her own excellent coordination.

"What's down here?" Theo asked.

"Believe it or not, more storage. Victor uses it for some of his old gear. The stuff he didn't want to risk science camp attendees or future bed-and-breakfast guests finding."

"Like what?" Theo nearly ran into Essa as the other girl stopped abruptly.

Essa lit a match, then touched it to an old-fashioned lantern on the floor of the tunnel. The flickering yellow light revealed a metal cage in front of them. It was big enough for a gorilla, maybe even big enough for a giant ground sloth, were such things not extinct and therefore impossible to cage. It wasn't old like the lantern, though. It was sleek and shiny. On the open door there was a keypad instead of a regular lock.

"Like that," Essa said.

"Whoa. What's it for? Why does he have it down here? And what does it have to do with my parents?"

"See for yourself, Theo." Essa stepped aside, gesturing for Theo to go in.

It was still too dark to see much of anything. Theo picked up the lantern, holding it out as she stepped into the cage and searched for what was inside. Some sort of writing, or another clue. She shined it on the far side, glanced up at the top of the cage, and then down at the bottom. "I don't see—" Then she froze and looked back at Essa. "You called me Theo."

Essa shut the cage door. A beep sounded as the latches slammed into place. Essa stood on the other side of the bars, staring folornly at Theo, her big hazel eyes flickering with the reflection of the lantern.

"Essa," Theo said, trying to keep her voice even. "This isn't funny. Let me out."

"I'm sorry," Essa said. "Really, I am. You'll be safe, and I promise I won't keep you in there for long. But I can't let you all leave yet. This way, they'll stay. Alexander and Wil and your friends would never leave you behind." Essa's smile was somehow angry and sad at the same time. "You're not superfluous to them. You're lucky."

She knew all their names. Maybe she had this whole

time. Essa had tricked them and tricked Theo straight into a trap. Theo set down the lantern, then launched herself at the cage door. It didn't budge under her assault. She tried to reach the keypad, but it was angled away from the open bars, yet another lock she couldn't pick.

"Let me out!" Theo shouted. "I trusted you! I liked you! And this whole time, you've been working with Edgaren't?"

Essa snorted a laugh. "He told me you all call him that. So cute. But no, silly goose. I'm not working for him." Essa took a step back, the pool of light no longer illuminating her. She became nothing but a receding glow as she said one final thing that made Theo terrified for Alexander and everyone else obliviously getting ready for bed upstairs.

"*He's* working for *me*."

CHAPTER
TWENTY-ONE

Theo shouted. She yelled until her voice went scratchy and raw. But she had an excellent sense of distance and space, and she knew she was too far beneath the manor for any hope of being heard. Air didn't vibrate long enough to carry her voice up to anyone who would help her.

She tried throwing herself against the bars, but other than bruising her shoulder, it didn't do anything. This cage was designed for something or someone much bigger and stronger than she was.

Theo was stuck.

Absolutely, completely stuck.

Her bees swarmed her entire body, making

her want to buzz right out of her skin. She was livid, she was furious, she was enraged, and she was also sad and hurt and worried and scared. She had too many feelings and nothing to do with any of them.

What would Alexander do if he were with her? No. What would *she* do if it were *Alexander* here? She'd do anything to find him. Just like she had done everything she could at Camp Creep to get him back when he was trapped beneath all that braindye.

Theo took a deep breath. She would do anything to help Alexander, and she knew *he* would do anything to help her. No matter what Essa told the others, no matter what was happening in the manor above them, Theo trusted that Alexander would know something was wrong. Because he was Alexander, and he was always sure that something was wrong.

She hoped he trusted himself this time, because she was trusting him. That, somehow, through twintuition or instincts or just a stomachache that he couldn't ignore, he would know. He would look for her. He wouldn't give up, the way she didn't give up at Camp Creek.

She wished there was some way she could help him, something she could do to guide him. But all the lantern showed her was the bars of her cage, the cave around her, and the rocks littering the cave floor.

Sound waves are funny, Essa said in her memory.

Theo grinned in grim determination, reaching as far as she could between the bars, hoping her fingers found what they needed.

CHAPTER
TWENTY-TWO

Everyone had showered and changed. Lucy was wearing a white nightdress whose sleeves draped down like bat wings. Edgar wore a pair of Wil's flannel pj pants and one of her cool T-shirts— unsurprisingly, he managed to pull off the style with flare, though he did keep trying to adjust a tie or kerchief that wasn't there. Henry had chosen one of Theo's tank tops and a pair of Alexander's swim trunks as pajamas. No one knew why, and no one wanted to ask and risk upsetting him since he seemed content.

They were all content, actually, eating warm cookies while wearing cozy pj's and telling stories in front of a roaring fire as a storm raged harmlessly outside. It was a perfect recipe for contentedness that not even Alexander's mom could have improved on.

No, that wasn't true. He sighed. If his parents were here—if all their parents were here—then it would be the actual perfect recipe for contentedness. He didn't want to tell Essa that, though, since she seemed so competitive about his mother's recipes.

"And that's when they opened the car door and found a hook, hanging on the handle!" Edgar said with a flourish. "And that's why I should never be allowed to go fishing again!" he added to general laughter. It wasn't a scary story at all, but Edgar was a good storyteller.

"Wil, do you have a scary story?" Mina asked.

Wil didn't look up from Rodrigo. The glow of it lit her face from beneath in classic spooky lighting style. "It's called . . . 'The Day the Battery Died.'"

Alexander didn't think it sounded spooky at all, and he was glad. He didn't like scary stories. He understood why other people might choose to be frightened on purpose, but wasn't he scared often enough as it was?

"What do you think?" Essa asked quietly as Wil told a harrowing tale of her phone battery being in the red and no chargers in sight. Essa was sitting on the floor next to Alexander, her arms around her knees as she watched him eat a cookie. "Better than your mom's?"

Alexander smiled at her. He didn't want to tell her the truth, because his mom's cookies were still better. But she'd had so many more years to perfect them. He was sure Essa would get there someday. "These are great. Why are you so competitive with her, anyway?" Obviously, Alexander was used to people being extremely competitive over strange things—he had yet to eat a meal faster than Theo in their entire life, since she decided speed eating was a thing she needed to be good at—but he was curious why Essa seemed fixated on this.

"Where are our shoes and socks?" Henry interrupted. His shower had at last fully cleaned his hair, and they were all shocked to discover it was so blond it was almost white. But, since glitter is a supernaturally evil force not even science could account for, he still had sparkles all over. "My feet are cold."

"Yeah, I don't like being without my boots unless I'm sleeping," Quincy said.

"They were soaking wet," Essa answered, "and they'd never dry on a chilly night like this. I put them near a heater in one of the guest rooms. I'll bring them back down when they're ready."

"Where's your luggage?" Henry demanded of Alexander. "I'm taking some socks!" He took a deep breath, then said in a calmer voice, "I'd like to borrow some socks, please. Because we're friends, and friends do nice things for each other but also ask for things in a nice way."

Alexander turned around to point his out. They had lined up all the suitcases and backpacks against the wall near the back entrance. Quincy's suitcase, Mina and Lucy's traveling trunk, Wil's backpack, Theo's suitcase, and his suitcase. His suitcase, where they had shoved all the family books. His suitcase, which was no longer against the wall.

Alexander stood, his heart racing. "Where's my suitcase? Did anyone move it?"

Wil stopped her story. They all rushed around the room, checking behind and under the two couches, throwing pillows aside, and searching the bathroom they'd all taken turns showering in. The suitcase was nowhere to be seen. And neither, for that matter, was . . .

"Theo!" Alexander said, then caught himself. "Theeold Dora! Has anyone seen Dora since she left to take a shower?" Maybe Theo had taken the suitcase to work on cracking the locks. But why wouldn't she tell him? And why wouldn't she reclaim her timer? He clutched it where it hung around his neck under his shirt.

A few weeks ago, he would have assumed Theo was mad and being immature or petty or reckless. But after what they'd been through, he meant it when he said he trusted her to be careful. Something was wrong. Maybe it was twintuition, or instincts, or just a sudden stomach-ache that was his body's way of telling him to be on alert, but he *knew* Theo hadn't wandered off.

Essa looked troubled. "I saw her in the kitchen, but she didn't have that suitcase. What did it have inside?"

"Books," Wil said, her glower downright dangerous. "*My* books, our books, which we worked very hard for."

"Books?" Essa's expression changed from troubled to alarmed. "Someone took your books?"

"It's fine," Wil snapped, trying to get her temper under control. "We'll find them. Where's Mr. Frank? We'd like to talk to him. I have a feeling he knows where Dora and the books are."

"Oh, he's been in his room all night. I don't think he has anything to do with this." Essa twisted some of her hair around one finger. "I probably should have said something, but when I saw her, Dora seemed upset. She said she was mad at all of you for not listening to her, and was going to hide to teach you a lesson. I thought she was playing a game. It seemed harmless. Just regular twelve-year-old stubborn pouting. You know how she is."

"Yeah, I guess," Wil said, tugging on one of her braids. "She can be a real twerp sometimes."

Alexander narrowed his eyes. Something was wrong. Essa was watching Wil carefully, so she didn't notice Alexander watching her.

A jolt of fear struck him like an electric shock. Essa was *pretending*. She was playing a part and watching for their reactions, like they had been doing to her with their fake names and their fake stories about their parents. They thought they had been tricking her, but what if she had been *letting* them trick her this whole time? Because she knew exactly what they were doing and it played perfectly into what she wanted?

This whole time, Essa had been pretending to be nothing more than a happy, bubbly teenage girl. He had noticed her flashes of terrible anger, her bouts of deep sadness, and the way she snapped right out of them as soon as anyone noticed. He'd tried not to pry, since he was used to Theo, who also got mad a lot.

A fact Essa was trying to use to trick them now. But if Theo was mad at them, they'd know about it. She might not always understand her emotions, or express them well, but she didn't try to hide them. Theo didn't hide anything. Not from him. He could imagine her dragging the books away to work on them in a last-ditch effort to save the day, but . . . he couldn't imagine her leaving him out of that plan. They were a team, now more than ever.

Whatever was going on here, wherever Theo was, Alexander didn't believe for a second she was hiding from them out of spite. And he had a feeling Essa knew where she was, or at least had an idea.

"I can help look for her," Essa said brightly. "We'll make a game of it."

"Thank you," Alexander said. He looked right at Wil. "We should find her fast, because my sister's afraid of the dark. Right, Willow?"

Wil frowned. "She's—" Then she noticed Alexander's raised eyebrow. Alexander felt a rush of relief that, at last, Wil was paying attention to them. Enough attention to catch on that Alexander was saying something deliberately and extremely false to signal that something was wrong. "Right. Super afraid of the dark. Essa, could you go get flashlights? In case the power goes out or we have to look in places that don't have lights?"

"Of course!" Essa bounced away, humming to herself.

"No way Theo's hiding," Alexander whispered. "Something is up. Mr. Fake must have gotten to Essa. We're on our own to help Theo."

"But Theo was mad at us," Henry said. "And when I was mad at Camp Creek, I always crawled away and hid in dark places. And I was *always* mad, so I was *always* hiding."

"Yeah, but you and Theo aren't the same. Everyone handles things in different ways. Theo wouldn't take the books without telling us. She wouldn't do anything that would make me worry. Not on purpose, anyway. She does a lot of things that make me worry all the time, but never to be mean. When Essa comes back, we'll tell her we're going to let Theo stay hiding until she's not mad anymore. But then, Mina, you make a big deal over the fact that Lucy's missing, too. It won't be hard to believe, because Lucy's always missing."

"That's true," a tiny voice said from the darkness somewhere above them.

"Good girl," Mina said. "Stay hidden, even when I'm calling for you."

"Mina and Edgar, you take Essa deep inside the manor looking for Lucy. Stall her as much as possible, and keep an eye out for Mr. Fake. The rest of us will stay here like we're not going to bother looking for Theo. And then when the coast is clear, we'll spread out and find her. Something bad is going on here, and I don't know what it is or who's behind it, but—"

"But Theo would find us," Quincy said, adjusting her hat like she was ready to get to work. "Even when Theo was angry with me, she didn't leave me to be lost to the braindye. She found me, brought me back to myself. Theo has our backs, and we have hers."

"What about the books?" Henry asked.

Wil surprised Alexander again. "The books don't matter. Theo is the priority."

"Team SOS has this covered." Quincy looped one of her lassos through the air, spelling out the letters *SOS* to emphasize them.

"I'm going to get so mad at whoever's behind this." Henry's voice quivered with barely contained rage.

"We'll keep Essa busy and buy you as much time as you need," Edgar said, grimly determined.

Just then, Essa reappeared. "I could only find a couple of flashlights. I thought we'd start on the second floor, going room by room."

Wil held out her hand, and Essa tossed the flashlight. Wil snatched it out of the air without even looking. She had her eyes on her phone like she was unbothered by the events of the night, like Theo had already slipped her mind.

Alexander sighed. "That's okay. I don't think we should waste our time. I'm sure you're right and she's hiding to bug us. Best thing we can do is ignore her until she gets bored. It won't take long. She gets bored fast if she's not moving, and she'll come back. There's nothing to worry about."

Essa's eyes narrowed. "That doesn't sound like you. You find a lot of things to worry about."

Alexander shrugged. "If she wants to be mad, I can't stop her. I'm going to try to get some sleep."

"Me too." Quincy yawned exaggeratedly.

Henry did the same, throwing himself onto a pile of pillows. "She can stay where she is! I *hate* it when people have bad attitudes!" he shouted, burrowing beneath the pillows until he was hidden from view.

Wil settled back down on the nearest couch, scrolling through her phone. "If Dora wants to pout, let her pout. It's annoying."

"Oh, dear!" Mina said, putting a hand against her heart. "Susy! She's wandered off again. Poe, Essa, would you two mind helping me look for her? I'm worried she'll curl up somewhere and fall asleep and we won't find her until the morning. I won't be able to sleep a wink, worrying about her."

Essa frowned at Alexander and Wil. "You're sure you don't want to look for Theo?"

Alexander froze, glad he was already looking down at his pillow. Essa called her Theo, not Dora. He shook his head, trying to keep his tone calm as he pretended like he hadn't noticed. "No. She can take care of herself." He lay down on the floor and pulled his pillow over his face so his expression wouldn't betray him. His head pressed against the stone tiles as Mina and Edgar drew Essa away. Alexander's heart was beating so loudly, he was shocked Essa couldn't hear it from the second floor.

"Okay," Henry hissed. "The coast is clear. Where should we start?"

But Alexander wasn't listening to him. He wasn't listening to his own pounding heart anymore, either. He was listening to something else. *Two* somethings else, both equally strange, and both coming to his ear through the floor itself. The first was the crash of the ocean, which shouldn't be audible from here. And the second was the distant but unmistakable Morse code of dot-dot-dot, dash-dash-dash, dot-dot-dot.

"SOS," he whispered.

CHAPTER
TWENTY-THREE

Wil lifted her head from where she had it pressed against the stone floor. "Maybe the basement," she said, whipping out Rodrigo and typing so quickly her fingers were a blur. "What's the address of this manor?" she muttered.

Quincy was already standing, lasso pointing the way. "I know where the basement door is; I can show you."

"Hang on. I'm getting the blueprints. All buildings have to receive approval before they're constructed, or when they're remodeled to, say, make a bed-and-breakfast out of a manor. The information is usually stored in local city databases. Give me a second to hack and bypass all the security."

Henry's eyes went wider than Quincy's lasso loop. "You can do that?"

"Please," Wil said, "it's local government, not secret international databases. I could do this in my sleep. Actually, I have once or twice. Done it in my sleep, I mean. Okay, the basement is only under the portion of the house closest to the road, so the part of the floor we're listening to is over . . . solid rock." Wil looked up from her phone, puzzled. "How are we hearing her tapping through solid rock?"

"She could be tapping on the walls of the basement," Henry said.

"But tapping on basement walls doesn't explain the sound of the ocean. Unless . . ." Alexander's stomach dropped. He knew *exactly* what he was hearing. "Sea caves," he whispered.

"What?" Wil was already standing to go break into the basement.

"There are sea caves in the cliff. Theo and I saw a trail down to them. But it's dangerous. The sign said not to go."

"You think Theo went into the dangerous sea caves alone? That's just like her." Wil let out an exasperated huff.

"No, it's not." Alexander was certain of it. Theo would never have gone into the sea caves on her own. She was brave, yes, but she wasn't reckless anymore. And she definitely wouldn't have done something that dangerous without telling anyone, or bringing Alexander along. If Theo was in the sea caves, she wasn't there by choice. "We have to rescue her."

"But—"

"There's no time for buts."

"Butts," Quincy said with a giggle, then got serious again. "Sorry."

Alexander pointed. "Quincy and Henry, you two break into the basement and look there just in case. I'll be right back." Alexander sprinted up the stairs to the main science room, luckily not running into Essa and the others. The charts he had studied earlier were all still there.

He held his breath as he ran his finger down the tidal patterns. "Low tide," he whispered, with a mixture of relief and terror. Because low tide meant they could get into the sea caves. But it also meant . . . they could get into the sea caves.

Rolling up the charts and bringing them along, he ran downstairs. "Come on," he said to Wil. "We don't have long before the tide starts rising. We have to hurry."

"Good luck, y'all. Be careful," Quincy said.

"You better not mess this up!" Henry shouted, but Alexander understood Henry was only yelling because he was worried. Alexander was worried, too.

He didn't want to do this. It went against everything he was. He'd have to walk past a sign telling him not to go into a place. He'd have to choose to expose himself to extreme danger. And he'd have to ask Wil to walk into that danger, too. Alexander's worst fears were all based around danger to himself, but also danger to the people he loved.

"Come on." Wil looked fierce and brave as she tucked Rodrigo into her pocket. Unexpectedly, her expression turned stricken. She pulled her phone back out and solemnly gave it to Quincy. "I can't risk it getting wet. If you find anything, text Edgar."

In order to save their sister, Alexander was throwing caution to the wind. Or at least, carefully and gently setting his caution aside where it could easily be reached again. And Wil was willingly giving up her phone. The Sinister-Winterbottoms had each other's backs, no matter what.

Wil held out her hand to Alexander. It wasn't the same as holding Theo's hand, but Alexander appreciated it nonetheless. "Let's go save our sister."

Together, they ran to the back door and flung themselves into the storm. It thrashed the coastline, the rain relentless, the waves pounding. Alexander tried not to think about the waves and the ocean and the fact that he was about to enter caves that would eventually let that very ocean in after him.

"We have thirty minutes," he shouted as they cautiously trekked down the path. Wil's flashlight barely helped. They were only in their socks—they hadn't even considered taking the time to look for their shoes. "So we have to make sure we're either out by then or are deep enough into the caves that the water won't reach us. If that's even possible." He very much hoped for the previous option.

"Okay!" Wil shouted back. "But, oh no! I don't have Rodrigo! How will we know how much time we have left?"

Alexander paused. It was a crucial mistake, not having something that could tell them the time. Then he remembered: he had a piece of Theo hanging around his neck to help and guide them.

He put his free hand around her timer. It gave him a boost of bravery. Having something Theo loved reminded him that Theo loved *him*, too, and trusted him. Theo had learned to be more cautious in order to help him. He could take some of her bravery into his own heart to help her. "I have it covered!" He pressed the button on top, and the timer began.

They barely found the turnoff for the sea caves path. Alexander didn't look at the sign warning them to absolutely not go that way, because he was too worried he'd agree with the sign if he read it again and lose all the courage he was trying so hard to hold on to.

Even though it was low tide, the waves were closer to the cliff than he wanted them to be. The beach was only a narrow strip of false protection. A liminal space, Essa had called this area. Not one world, and not the other.

But how would he know where the border was in the caves, where the line of safety appeared? Where they were officially out of reach of the ocean?

"There!" Wil pointed. Sure enough, a cave entrance gaped, a circle of even darker black in the middle of the dark storm.

"The cold, unknowable sea," Alexander whispered, hoping against hope that this cave wouldn't turn into a terrible wave pool while they were still inside it.

CHAPTER
TWENTY-FOUR

As Wil and Alexander took their first steps into the gaping maw of the sea caves entrance, Alexander pulled out Theo's timer and checked it. Five minutes had already passed.

"We have twenty-five minutes to either get deep enough in that we're above the water or to get out."

Wil looked around with the flashlight. The entrance tunnel was wide and flat, not sloping quickly up like Alexander had hoped. And, even worse, it led to not one but three tunnels. Each of which might lead to even more tunnels. He pictured the cliff like an ant farm, riddled with tunnels connecting to tunnels connecting to dead ends.

He didn't want to think about dead ends right now. He didn't want to think about anything involving the word *dead* at all. He'd even take the Sanguine Spa's vampire-bat-filled caves over these ones.

"We go left every time," Wil said. "Pick one direction and stick with it. That way we always know what direction we chose, in case there are options. That was what Theo said about mazes, right?"

Alexander nodded, surprised Wil remembered. She had been stuck with her nose in Rodrigo the first time they went through the hedge maze to get to the Sanguine Spa. But it made Alexander feel better. Between using Theo's plan to get through mazes and also her timer, it was almost like she was guiding them.

They took the tunnel on their left. Fortunately, it didn't curve far before ending abruptly in a solid wall of stone. They scurried back through it.

The middle tunnel was waiting. Alexander could feel the seconds ticking by. Literally feel them, each one a tiny tap against his chest from the timer. Alexander and Wil hurried as fast as they could, though the pebble-strewn ground hurt their feet and Wil's dim flashlight could only illuminate the area a few feet ahead of them. This tunnel, too, ended after a few twists and turns. None of which were leading them upward.

Back at the mouth of the cave, the first few rogue waves began lapping at the entrance.

"We can't spend much longer here or we'll be trapped," Wil said.

Alexander gestured, and they rushed into the third tunnel. It was hard to tell whether it was gradually ascending, or whether he only wanted it to be. They scrambled up and over rocks, then back down so often he couldn't keep track of whether they were higher overall than they had been at the mouth of the caves. Theo would have been able to tell, but Alexander wasn't good at understanding spaces like she was.

"How much longer do we have?" Wil asked, her voice as nervous as Alexander had ever heard it. She shined the light on the timer.

"Five minutes." Alexander stared down at the passing seconds, his heart pounding.

"I think we should go back," Wil said. "We can't risk getting caught below the high-tide mark, and we have no way of telling how far the tide will reach."

Alexander hated the idea of retreating. He took a step

forward, trying to pierce the darkness with his eyes. But instead of his eyes doing the piercing, something sharp pierced his foot. "Ow." He hopped on his other foot, which made that poor foot hurt, too. The tiny rocks on the cave floor were so painful to walk on.

He frowned. Tiny rocks. "Flash the light down here." The cave floor was shiny and dark, everything the same nearly black gray. But . . . Alexander pulled out his magnifying glass and crouched. "These aren't rocks; they're shells!" He remembered the tiny shells in Essa's hand. "The liminal-space markers! If we can get past where these are, we'll be above the tide line."

"We'll give it three more minutes," Wil said, "and then we run back."

Alexander agreed. They raced along the tunnel, Alexander using his magnifying glass to check the walls for the tiny shells. Soon, the line of shells along the walls dropped from the ceiling, to Alexander's eye level, to his belly button. "The shells are going down! I think we're beating the high-tide line!" Their path was still going up and down along the tunnel passageway's twists and turns, but he was confident it was more up than down now. A few tunnels branched away, but a quick check showed they had more shells than their current pathway.

Alexander thought they were still on the right track to get above the incoming water—and, hopefully, to find Theo.

"Look!" Alexander ran his soggy socks over the floor of the cave, then knelt down. The magnifying glass revealed only a few shell stragglers. There were hardly any left.

"What's the time?"

Alexander looked down. "Thirty-five minutes," he said softly. They had missed the window of opportunity. They couldn't go back now.

Wil put a hand on his shoulder. "We're safe, at least. Above the water. And Theo's been gone since before the tide was its lowest, so she couldn't be anywhere the water would reach her."

With a sigh of relief and a burst of determined confidence, they continued forward. Even if they were trapped in these caves now until the tide finished rising and then receded, they were safe. Ish. They scrambled over rocks and squeezed through narrow passageways. It wasn't fun or pleasant. It was cold and damp and loud, with the waves crashing into the lower cave tunnels and echoing angrily around them.

But it wasn't so loud that Alexander didn't hear the moment something changed. "Listen," he said.

"Morse code! We're coming, Theo!" Wil said. She and

Alexander ran, scrambling and climbing and squeezing and even crawling in a few places until at last they came around a bend to find the tunnel wider and higher than it had been before. Wider and higher *and* featuring one very big cage with one very small Theo inside.

She was lit by the lantern, sitting cross-legged against the edge of the cage, a rock in her hand smacking SOS against the wall of the cave.

"Because those vibrations traveling through rock would make it up to the manor when her voice traveling through the air wouldn't!" Alexander said, deeply proud of his smart sister.

"Theo!" Wil shouted. "You absolute twerp! We were so worried!"

Theo dropped the rock and rushed to the door of the cage. They ran to meet her there. To Alexander's puzzlement, Theo looked relieved, but there was no surprise on her face.

Theo grinned at them. "I knew you'd figure it out and come for me. You were even faster than I thought you'd be."

Alexander's chest swelled, his heart bursting with happiness and pride. He'd done it. He'd known his sister well enough to know she would never hide from him, and he'd been brave enough to figure out where she was and how to get to her. He pulled the timer off and passed it through the bars to her. "This helped."

Theo put it back around her own neck with relief. "Thank goodness I gave it to you, then. Now, get me out of here and let's go get Essa."

"Essa?" Wil asked, frowning at the keypad. "Alexander said we couldn't trust her."

"Yup." Theo's scowl could have lit the lantern all on its own, it was so fiery. "She's the one who locked me in here. We've been worried about Edgaren't showing up— it turns out *he's* working for *her*."

"What? Really?" Alexander couldn't believe it. Sure, he had suspected Essa, but that didn't make sense. What would Essa want with the books, or their parents? And why was a grown-up like Edgaren't working for a teenage girl? Edgaren't had been in the photo with their parents, so his connection to them made sense. Maybe Essa was his daughter?

But that raised the question again: why would he be working for her?

"This is going to take me ages to crack," Wil grumbled.

"You break codes all the time," Theo said, bouncing impatiently.

"No, I *hack* codes all the time. This is different." Will was pushing buttons to get a feel for how the code pad worked. "I don't have the right equipment. I don't even know how many numbers the code is."

"What about Mr. Fake?" Alexander asked.

"Mr. Fake," Theo said, her eyes going wide.

"Yeah, exactly. Mr. Fake. He must be helping Essa, too. We've got to get the others out of there."

"Mr. Fake!" Theo said.

"Yeah, I know."

"*Mr. Frank!*" Theo shouted, pointing behind Alexander and Wil.

They turned to see the enormous man lurching through the cave right toward them.

"You can't have my sisters!" Alexander shouted, throwing himself in front of Wil and Theo. No one could believe he did it, especially Alexander himself. But it didn't matter. Mr. Frank simply lifted him up and set him aside, then brushed past Wil.

He grabbed hold of the cage door, let out a terrible roar, and ripped it clean off its hinges.

CHAPTER
TWENTY-FIVE

Mr. Frank's chest heaved from effort as he tossed aside the cage door.

Theo was free. And very, very confused. "Wait, you're . . . helping us?" she asked, picking up the lantern. Alexander rushed to her side, checking to make sure she was okay. Wil looked in the direction Mr. Frank had come from.

"There's another way out?" Wil asked.

"In the basement," Theo said. "That's how we got in."

Mr. Frank nodded.

"So, you're *not* on Edgaren't and Essa's side," Alexander said, wanting to be sure. "But that doesn't make any sense! The real Mr. Frank is dead. I saw the death certificate."

Mr. Frank put a hand over his heart. "I'm the real Mr. Frank."

"So, the death certificate was fake?"

"No, it's real."

"So, you're . . . a ghost?"

Mr. Frank's heavy eyebrows raised. "What? No. Ghosts aren't real."

"Oh, boy, do we have news for you," Wil muttered.

"If the death certificate's real, then how are you—" Theo shook her head. "We don't have time for this. Are you on Essa's side or not?"

Mr. Frank shook his head. His voice was still a deep, unnerving rumble, and he was still enormous and glowery. But he gestured for them to follow him safely out of the caves. "I tried to warn you all, but you didn't listen to me."

Theo felt a stab of guilt. Mr. Frank looked scary and Essa looked sweet, and because of it, they had all suspected him from the start. "In our defense," she said, "the last few adults in charge of the places we went were all . . ." She drifted off, looking for the right word.

"Annoying," Wil said.

"Nefarious," Alexander said, which was a word that meant "wicked" and "mean in clever ways."

"Annoyingly nefarious and little bit monstrous," Theo finished.

Mr. Frank's huge shoulders drooped. "I know how I look, how I sound. It's hard for people to like me sometimes, unless they get to know me. And because I couldn't speak with you all—Essa was always watching, always catching me—I decided the best thing I could do to protect you was try to scare you away. Since you were scared of me anyway. When people assume you're a monster, sometimes it's easiest to pretend to be one."

"That's not fair to you," Alexander said, genuinely regretful. "I'm sorry we judged you."

"I'm sorry I couldn't tell you the truth. Essa threatened me."

"What did she threaten you with?" Theo couldn't imagine what a teenage girl could possibly do to humongous Mr. Frank.

"Victor." Mr. Frank let out a long, sad sigh. "He's my best friend. Earlier this summer, he disappeared in the middle of the night. When I started looking for him, Essa showed up. She said if I wanted to see Victor again, I had to give her full control of the manor and stay out of her way. I tried to sabotage the camp to keep kids from coming, but that didn't work. I didn't want to help her, but I didn't know what else to do. I couldn't go openly against her and risk losing my chance to get Victor back. Victor's always seen the real me. He helped me be a person again after my relationship with Agnes—"

"Who?" Theo asked.

"The fake Mrs. Widow," Wil explained.

"Yes, after Agnes tricked me, broke my heart, stole my inheritance, and caused an accident that left me in pieces."

"Emotionally?" Alexander asked.

"No," Mr. Frank said. They had reached a dead end, their path forward blocked by something. Mr. Frank reached up to move it. His sleeve slipped up his arm, revealing careful, neat surgical scars. "Literally."

"She . . . literally left you in pieces?"

"Yes. And Victor fixed me."

"Wait—Victor fixed you from being dead? To being . . . not dead?"

Mr. Frank shrugged. "He's very smart. Come on. We have to get the others and get you somewhere safe.

I shouldn't have let Essa have her way. Victor wouldn't want that. Not at the expense of your safety."

"*Literally in pieces.* Every time I think things can't get weirder around here," Theo muttered.

Alexander shivered in disgust as he scooted past the moldy mattress, contorting his body so he wouldn't touch it. Theo smiled affectionately. She had been right that Alexander would never have found the hidden entrance if it meant touching that thing. She couldn't believe he had gone through the sea caves, in spite of the warning sign. She was so proud of him.

She was proud of Wil, too. But something was off; something was strange about her sister. "Wait, where's Rodrigo?" Theo asked.

Wil twitched, her fingers holding the phantom shape of a phone. "I left it behind so we could find you."

Theo gasped and threw her arms around Wil. "I really am your favorite! I knew it!"

Wil patted her on top of her head. "You remain in my top-four family members, as always."

"Where can we go to be safe?" Alexander asked, because that was his top priority. His feet squished along the basement floor, leaving wet sock footprints. "We can leave in the van, but we don't have the books, and—"

"I have the books," Mr. Frank said. "I saw Essa looking in the suitcase and smiling, so I knew it was something she wanted. I took them earlier, while she was distracted. I'm sorry if it made you worry."

"Thank goodness!" Theo did a twirl in giddy relief. "I think I finally have the locks figured out. I only need one more thing."

"What's that?" Alexander asked.

"A way to look closer." Theo smiled at him. "I realized down in the cage, because I had time to think about the Stein book. I was trying to get them open without reading the instructions."

"You do that a lot."

"I do! I hate reading the instructions. But I looked closer at the lock, and there's tiny writing all around it. So . . ."

"My magnifying glass!" Alexander reached into his pocket and handed it over. Theo tucked it into her borrowed jacket pocket, next to the Stein book.

Mr. Frank unlocked the door to the stairs and opened it. A rope shot out and looped around him. Quincy and Henry leaped into view. "Got you, villain! Now tell us where our—" Quincy stopped. "Oh. I guess we know where our friends are."

"He's on our side," Wil said, holding out her hand. Quincy handed over Rodrigo. Wil stroked the phone lovingly, sent a quick thumbs-up text to Edgar.

"Theo!" Quincy practically knocked Theo over with the force of her hug. And, even more surprisingly, Henry joined, squeezing them both.

"We were worried!" he shouted angrily.

"Thank you for worrying," Theo laughed as Henry let go of her. "I wasn't worried. Well, I was a little worried. But I knew you would all find me. And I know exactly where we should go to hide from Essa while we decide our next move. The third floor."

"That's Victor's laboratory," Mr. Frank said with a scowl. "He doesn't like people in there."

"And it's the one place in the manor Essa's never been able to break into. She tried to get me to do it for her."

Alexander nodded. "Mr. Frank, you get the rest of the books. Wil, text Edgar to figure out an excuse to ditch Essa and meet us at the third floor with Mina and Lucy. Henry and Quincy, can you grab our bags so we're ready to go?"

"On it," Quincy said. "Oh. Uh, sorry." She flicked her wrist so the rope would release Mr. Frank, then raced up the stairs and turned down the hallway to the first-floor main room. Before Henry could even catch up to her, she was back, the suitcases and bags sliding across the floor, tugged along by Quincy's lasso. They each grabbed a bag and followed Mr. Frank up.

Halfway along the servant stairs to the second floor, he reached up and moved a panel of the ceiling out of the way. Alexander's suitcase was tucked up there. "Tall-people hiding place," Mr. Frank said.

"Wow, I'll bet you can also see the top of the fridge without standing on a chair," Theo said in admiration.

But the books weren't the only things in the tall people hiding place. A tiny bundle of white tumbled free, landing in Mr. Frank's arms.

Lucy gave him a small smile, patting his cheek. Mr. Frank's whole face shifted in surprised and tender shock at receiving affection from a little kid. He was still huge and hulking, but there was a gentleness there that they had all been too afraid of him to notice. He shifted Lucy so she was riding on his shoulders—her blond hair almost brushing the ceiling—which freed up his hands to carry Alexander's suitcase.

Alexander turned to Wil, but she wiggled Rodrigo at him. "Already texted Edgar and Mina that we found Lucy."

At the top of the stairs, Theo watched as Mr. Frank

held up a hand and waved it in a semicircle. The door, which had no lock or handle, and therefore no way for Theo to pick it, swung open.

"Magic?" she gasped.

"Magnets," Mr. Frank said, holding up his wrist. A thick metal bracelet was there. "It lets me slide the dead bolt open and shut from this side."

"Genius!"

"Victor *is* a genius. He wanted to make sure no guests could ever accidentally get into the laboratory." Mr. Frank ushered them in.

Mina and Edgar raced up the stairs after them. "We shut Essa in a broom closet and ran!" they said, gasping. Mr. Frank waited for them to get in, then shut and bolted the door.

"We're safe." Alexander breathed a sigh of relief. He turned and took in the room. Or rather, the laboratory. He felt much less safe than he had mere seconds before. It was filled with all sorts of equipment and medical devices. The center had a metal operating table surrounded by wires and cords, all plugged in like it was recharging a battery. And above them, directly below the roof lightning rod, there was an enormous metal orb. It hummed, glowing faintly.

"What is this place?" Theo asked.

"Frogs," Lucy said quietly, pointing. Sure enough, there was an entire aquarium filled with frogs.

"That's how Victor perfected his process." Mr. Frank lowered Lucy to the floor. "He'd rescue dead frogs and then fix them."

"How do you fix dead— Nope. No time for that," Theo said. "Hand me the books!" She took the suitcase, pulled the books out, and sat on the floor, peering through the magnifying glass. "Aha! These *are* directions! I could have had these cracked so long ago." Resisting the urge to pull her hair in frustration at all her wasted time and effort, Theo read aloud to herself. "*The Boneless Skeleton Opens the Locks.*" She leaned back. "What is a boneless skeleton? A ghost?"

Alexander frowned. "If it's boneless, it's not a skeleton."

"Unless . . . ," Wil said, reaching into her pocket and pulling out the key with no teeth. "Unless the boneless skeleton is a skeleton key, without any prongs."

CHAPTER
TWENTY-SIX

"But wait," Theo said. "If that's the key we've needed this whole time—which explains why I couldn't pick the locks, because they aren't normal locks, and not because I'm not extremely good at picking locks, which I am—then what was that ring of little keys that Edgaren't took from us?"

Alexander looked at Lucy. She was perched on top of the frog enclosure, staring down at the amphibians with a hungry expression. "I got them from Lucy's nest," he said. "I assumed they were for the books, because the books were also at the spa, and the keys seemed like the right size."

Lucy shrugged and smiled secretively, keeping her little red mouth closed.

"You knew all along they weren't the right keys?" Theo gasped.

Lucy put a hand over her mouth, giggling. "You never asked."

Theo laughed, too. She couldn't even be mad now that they had the real solution. "You little rat!"

"Yes!" Lucy grinned, revealing her tiny, sharp fangs. "A rat!"

"Wait—wait—that's your sixth-favorite animal? I guessed it?" Theo jumped up in the air, fists raised. "I did it! I won! *I won!* I knew I would!"

Alexander put a hand on her shoulder. "Maybe we should focus on opening the books right now?"

"Oh, right. Yeah. That's more important." Theo said the words, and she knew they were true, but she couldn't help feeling like her best moment this entire summer was inadvertently winning Lucy's impossible game. "Rats," she whispered to herself, enjoying the taste of triumph.

Wil set the books in a row, taking them in with shining eyes. "I've waited so long for this."

"How did you know about the books in the first place?" Alexander asked. "You never told us."

"Why aren't we opening them?!" Henry shouted.

"Give us a minute!" Theo responded. "We've built up to this for a long time!"

Wil ignored Henry's impatience. "Ever since Mom and Dad left, I've been searching for information. Tracing their credit cards, their cell phones. When that didn't work, I started looking for relatives, anyone who might know where they were, anyone they might be staying with. Searching the Sinister name brought up old news articles from the summer we now know they were all at Camp Creek together. The articles mentioned that the missing teens were often seen reading and writing in family journals. The last time any of the witnesses saw the books, they were being held by Vlad Blood. Mina and Lucy's father."

"So that's why you were looking for them at the spa!"

Wil nodded. "I think they're family journals, kept over generations, and our parents were the most recent people to write in them. That summer when they were all together. That summer that links us all."

"But Essa gave you that key," Alexander said, troubled.

Theo shook her head. "No, Wil found it."

Wil also seemed puzzled. "Why would Essa want us to be able to open the books if she's Edgarent's boss? She must not have known what the key was."

"I think she's known more than any of us this whole time." Alexander stared down at the stack of books and the key, still held in Wil's hand. "Maybe we should—"

"I am going to explode if we don't open them right now!" Henry's face was a deep red to underscore his words.

Wil nodded with understanding. "Whatever Essa did or didn't know doesn't matter. We have the books and the key. So we're going to open them." She inserted the key into the Hyde book first, pressed it in, and . . .

There was a click. The lock released. The book opened.

Henry grabbed it, scanning the pages like he was starving and it was a banquet. But not a buffet, because Alexander didn't want to imagine a buffet under any circumstances.

"Well?" Theo prodded.

"It's a lot about two guys called Id and Ego, I think," Henry said. "Shh, I'm reading."

"Mine?" Quincy asked. Wil quickly unlocked the

Graves book and handed it to her, then the Blood book for Mina, then the Stein book and passed it to Mr. Frank, who held it reverently. Edgar took a deep breath and opened the Widow book, then started laughing.

"What?" Alexander asked, so nervous he could hardly stand it. He still didn't know whether or not they should have opened the books, but now that they had, he was desperate to know what was in them.

"It reads like a soap opera. A very dark and dramatic soap opera. Of course this is what my family wrote about." Edgar turned pages, a fond smile on his face.

"Mine's about the family business!" Quincy said, excited as she whirled through the pages, speed-reading. "Wow, I never saw that technique before!"

"Medical notes," Mr. Frank said softly. "Victor's family has a long history of scientific experimentation and advancement. Here, in the back, his own contributions—even when he was a teen, he was brilliant. My wonderful friend."

Wil paused, staring at the unopened Sinister book. It was last in line next to the unclaimed Siren book.

"Is it weird that I'm scared?" Wil whispered.

"It's never weird to be scared; I'm scared all the time," Alexander said. "But what if—what if we finally have the book open and it's not helpful? What if it's not what we need?"

Theo felt like she was going to erupt, a fountain of buzzing bee energy pouring out of her in a destructive torrent. She wanted the book open now. But also . . . she was scared of the same thing they were. "Open the Siren one first."

Wil popped open the Siren book. "Mom," she said softly.

"Mom's in the book?" Alexander asked.

Wil held up an old postcard tucked into the front. Someone had glued a photo to the front of it. It wasn't from when their parents were teens, though. Their mom in the photo was clearly pregnant, and she was holding little Wil's hand, both of them beaming. They were standing close, blocking the view of where they were. Next to their mom, with their arms around each other's shoulders, was a beautiful woman with long blue-black hair and enormous eyes. She wore a sparkly blue mermaid-style dress and winked at the camera.

Wil turned the postcard over. There was no return address, just a few scribbled lines and a barcode for purchase. "*Dearest Vladdy-Poo,*" she read, "*I know we're not supposed to see each other, but we couldn't resist this once.*

Thinking of you, wishing you were here—but at night, of course. And remember, all our secrets are safe here with me. XOXO Marina Siren." Wil looked up.

"Who is she?" Theo asked.

"If we can figure out who she is and where that photo was taken, then we can find her and get the answers!" Alexander said. "What else is on the postcard? Anything?"

"Nothing, just a stamp and this barcode. Oh," Wil said, then tipped her head back and laughed. "Oh, it's so obvious. I know exactly where she is!"

"Excellent," a sweet voice like the chime of silver said. Everyone in the laboratory turned, shocked, to see Essa standing in the very open doorway. "I knew you'd figure it out for me."

CHAPTER
TWENTY-SEVEN

"But you can't get in this room!" Theo said, outraged.

"Yes," Essa said. "That *would* be a clever thing to tell someone so that, if they started suspecting me, this was exactly where they'd go. I've explored this whole laboratory and had time to make some interesting changes to Victor's designs. Cue lightning." Essa pointed upward.

There was a deafening boom as thunder and lightning hit at exactly the same time. Everything went brilliantly white and then totally dark, and then brilliantly white once more. The giant metal orb beneath the lightning rod was crackling with energy.

"Science camp time! Electricity has to go somewhere," Essa said. "Normally it's diverted throughout the manor to provide power, but I made some adjustments." She flipped a switch on the wall. They had been so distracted by the laboratory and the books, they hadn't bothered looking at the floor or the ceiling. Essa had somehow put huge metal rings around the center of the room where they were all now standing. One ring on the ceiling, and one on the floor. There was a hum and a crackle, and then sparks and flashes all around them. They were trapped. Fingers of white energy formed cage bars that not even Mr. Frank could tear apart.

"Don't try to step over it," Essa said, her tone getting serious. "I have all your shoes, so you don't have any barrier between your bodies and the electrical currents."

"And bodies conduct electricity," Alexander said, eyeing the terrible streaks of light like if he stopped watching them they might reach out and grab him.

Theo's bees were silent. There was already enough humming and buzzing in the room to fill anyone. "This was exactly our plan," she said sadly. "To lure Edgaren't here and trap him. But Essa did it better." Theo's shoulders slumped. She was always competitive, always wanted to win, and she hadn't. She'd lost, because she had the players and rules all mixed up. "And she did give Wil the key on purpose, so we'd open the books and figure things out for her."

"Now, hey," Essa said, "don't look so defeated. I'm proud of both of you. Alexander, you used the information about tides and liminal spaces to get to Theo. I actually wasn't expecting that! And, Theo, you remembered about sound waves and used the rocks to carry your message up to Alexander. It was so hard not telling you how to use the key, when you were struggling to pick the book locks, but I knew you'd get there on your own with Wil's help. And you did! That's amazing. And don't think I'm not proud of the rest of you, too. You all worked together and looked out for each other. That says a lot. You deserve better than what you've had this summer. So please don't be scared. I promised you I wasn't going to let anything happen to you, and I meant it. As long as you stay where you are, you're totally safe."

"I disagree with your definition of *safe*," Alexander said, trying to stay as still as possible in the center of the room, imagining a dozen scenarios where he tripped on a frog and hit the electricity, or another lightning bolt hit and fried the circuits and made the bolts surge out to get them, or Quincy tried to lasso the orb and brought it crashing down on all of them. Which she was trying to do that very moment. He put a hand out on her arm and shook his head.

"I know it's not ideal," Essa said. "But I can't let you leave. I can't give up. Not when I'm this close to what I want."

"Who are you really?" Theo demanded. "*Did* you get braindyed at Camp Creek? Is that why you're doing this?"

"Why are you so interested in our parents?" Alexander asked, his voice soft. "In our mom? What do you want?"

"The same thing you all do: I want to find them. I've been trying for so long. And now we're going to find them together." She smiled, and she meant it. Alexander could tell. It wasn't a fake smile or a smile meant to hide how she was really feeling. Essa was genuinely *happy* right now. "I'm so glad we had a couple of days before you figured it out. It's been fun spending time with you all, getting to know you, and now you all know me, so you know you can trust me."

"What?" Theo said, aghast. "We'll never trust you again!"

"Didn't you like your time here, though? Didn't you feel safe, and seen, and valued? Didn't I make sure everything we did was something you needed? I gave you time to research, I gave you activities, I gave you information and science and food and fun. I ignored the fact that you were all lying to me the whole time, that you were being fake and not true. I didn't let it hurt my feelings. Because I care about you all." She beamed at Henry, who looked like he was ready to explode, much like his volcano. At Quincy, who was now trying to get her rope past the line of electricity to lasso the switch on the wall but couldn't quite make it. At Mina, who was holding tight to Lucy to make sure the little girl didn't go close to the dangerous edges. At Edgar, who was carefully gathering the books and packing them back in Alexander's suitcase, always on task even in an emergency. And at last, at Wil, Theo, and Alexander.

"I gave you the summer your parents didn't," Essa said.

"It was a lie, though," Alexander said.

"It wasn't." Essa looked hurt, which baffled Alexander. "I *know* you had fun with me, enjoyed spending time with me. And we'll keep spending time together as we find your parents, now that Wil's figured it out."

"I'm not going to tell you where they are." Wil folded her arms. "You can't make me do anything I don't want to do."

"That's true," Theo said. No one could budge Wil

when she got stubborn. When she was seven years old, their parents told her she couldn't play on the family computer until she cleaned her room. So, instead of cleaning her room, she took apart all the electronics in the house and built her own computer out of the parts. Their parents were so impressed, they agreed to let her room stay messy as long as she didn't destroy any more appliances.

"I think you'll change your mind," Essa said, "when you finally understand what the stakes are. You have no other options, anyway. No help. No—"

From deep in the house the doorbell rang with a terrible low toll.

"There he is," Essa said. "Late, as usual. I'm going to let our mutual friend in, and then we'll figure this all out. Don't worry." Essa turned and skipped down the stairs, singing, "Do you know the mustache man?" in a chillingly cheerful tone.

Mr. Frank put himself between the kids and the door. "I'll do what I can to help," he said. "I'm only sorry I didn't do more for you children."

"No, no, no." Wil stared down at the suitcase with the books inside. All the jostling of Alexander's suitcase had made the letter from their mom rise to the top. None of them had looked at it in a while. Wil picked it up. "I don't know what to do, Mom," she whispered. "I always know what to do, but not now." Then she looked at Alexander and Theo, her expression so desperate and worried that Alexander couldn't stand it.

"We'll be okay," he said, and he was surprised to find he meant it. Maybe it was because things had gotten so scary, so stressful, so weird, that he couldn't be any more worried than he already was. Or maybe he really had been able to learn some of Theo's tremendous bravery and take it inside himself. Either way, he nodded. "We'll be okay, because we're together."

"But we were never supposed to be here," Wil said, tugging on her braids. "This is my fault. Mom and Dad wanted us safe. They sent us to Aunt Saffronia to keep us *away* from all this, but I had to keep digging, had to keep looking. We should have gone back to Aunt Saffronia's house when she told us to, instead of going on to Camp Creek. Now we're out of options."

"If we had picked the safe option, Quincy and Henry wouldn't be okay," Alexander pointed out.

"And Mina and Lucy would have been lured to Camp Creek and changed, too," Theo said. "We might be stuck here, but at least we're stuck here together. And we're all ourselves. I like ourselves a lot."

Edgar put a gentle hand on Wil's shoulder. "You'll figure something out. I know you will."

"Yeah," Quincy said. "Y'all are the smartest, bravest kids I've ever known."

Mina was still holding Lucy away from the lightning bolts. "I believe in you, Sinister-Winterbottoms. There's nothing you can't do."

"I think we're dead meat!" Henry shouted.

"You shouldn't believe in me," Wil said, looking at Edgar with tears in her eyes. "I couldn't even figure out how to resummon Aunt Saffronia! Why didn't my mom leave us any useful information? I've been on my own this whole time. All she left was this silly, pointless letter." Wil shook it angrily.

Alexander took it from her, holding it carefully. "It wasn't pointless. It told me to be cautious, which has saved us. And it told Theo to be brave, which has saved us. And it told you to—" Alexander couldn't believe it. It was so obvious. So simple. "Wil! *Use your phone!*"

Wil frowned at Rodrigo, then let out a burst of laughter. "Oh, no, it really was that simple the whole time. I even have Aunt Saffronia's number programmed in. I didn't put it in there. Mom must have. I just needed to . . . call her." Wil dialed the number and put it on speakerphone.

It rang, and rang, and rang. "Come on," Wil muttered. "We *need* you."

"We really do," Alexander whispered.

"Please, Aunt Saffronia," Theo said.

"It's always more about intent than ceremony," a dreamy voice said. Between one blink and the next, Aunt Saffronia was standing beside Alexander and Theo. "People always get so hung up on the ceremony of it all. But you're Sinisters. You simply had to call and state what you needed."

"Aunt Saffronia!" Theo and Alexander said at once. They threw their arms around her, forgetting that she was a ghost. But she was solid enough to hug, so hug her they did.

She patted their heads awkwardly, her voice fond. "There, there. I have returned from the void, and we can set everything right now. We must hurry, though. As soon as they see me, I'll be dismissed again."

"But you can only be sent away by a family member," Edgar said, his black eyebrows drawn together. "That's what Charlotte told me. Be sent away by a family member, or lose your anchor to this plane of existence."

"Yes, exactly. Now, I can take only two at a time to my sanctuary, so we should—"

Footsteps were approaching up the stairs. A light set of small, cheery footsteps and a heavy set of large, mean footsteps.

"We're too late," Alexander whispered.

"Not quite," Quincy said. The others nodded at her and then at Wil.

Wil crouched in front of Alexander and Theo, looking them right in the eyes. "I love you, twerps." She shoved Alexander's suitcase full of books into his arms, tucked the skeleton key into Theo's pocket, then nodded at Aunt Saffronia. "Keep them safe!"

Aunt Saffronia put a hand on either twins' shoulders. It felt like walking through a spiderweb. "Wait," Theo said, realizing what Wil was saying.

"No!" Alexander shouted as the room twisted and spun. He was falling sideways, sucked through a vacuum, couldn't breathe but somehow also didn't need to, and then—

Alexander and Theo were sitting at the table in Aunt Saffronia's pleasantly old-fashioned kitchen. The walls were still a charming marigold orange, the floor tiles black-and-white checkerboard, the table set for three. And only three.

Their sister and all their friends were left behind, in the clutches of Essa and Edgaren't.

"What did you do?" Theo asked.

"Take us back!" Alexander demanded.

Aunt Saffronia sat across from them, her pale face placid and unmoved. "I'm sorry," she said. "But I'm bound to the will of the Sinister who summoned me. Which means I'm bound to Wil's will, which is powerful indeed. I have to keep you two safe. I have to keep you two here."

"Then go and get the rest of them!" Theo stood, throwing her chair across the room.

Rather than clattering to the ground or denting the wall, it was immediately back in front of the table where it had been. There was a window with filmy white curtains. Theo ran to it and shoved the curtains aside, but whatever was beyond the window was as filmy and white as the curtains themselves. The house wasn't cold—the temperature didn't feel like anything, in fact—but it *smelled* cold. Theo couldn't believe she didn't realize before that it wasn't a normal house at all.

Aunt Saffronia sighed. It sounded like a leaf falling to

the ground in the first autumn frost. "If I go back there, they'll be able to banish me again, and then you two will be trapped here. *Forever.* The only way we're all safe is if we're all here, together. Hidden. They can't banish me in my own sanctuary. And they can't get to you, either. I know you're unhappy, but Wil wanted you safe. Your parents wanted you safe."

Alexander swallowed hard. He looked at Theo. Theo looked at him. "We understand," he said. "But we can't be happy being safe when our sister and our friends aren't."

Aunt Saffronia nodded, her expression solemn and sad. "I am bound by what Wil wanted. But you are not. I'll do what I can to help you, without breaking her request."

"Good enough," Theo grumbled. "We really are happy to have you back."

Aunt Saffronia's pale, pale face shimmered into a smile. "I missed you, too."

"Well," Alexander said, grabbing his suitcase, which fortunately had come with them to . . . wherever they were now. "We have the books." Alexander piled them on the table. "And the key."

"And we have each other." Theo added the key to the pile.

Aunt Saffronia seemed to shimmer in and out when she saw it. "You need to stick together," she whispered.

"That was what Essa said, too," Alexander said with a frown. "And she said we needed more time, and we needed to look closer."

Theo nodded, adding her timer and Alexander's magnifying glass to the pile. "We'll figure it out."

Alexander took her hand in his, even though, surprisingly, he wasn't feeling scared. He and Theo were together, after all.

"We'll be cautious," she said.

"And we'll be brave," he added.

"And we'll save them all," Theo declared. Alexander squeezed her hand in agreement.

They just had no idea how they were going to do it.

ACKNOWLEDGMENTS

In 1818 a teenage girl named Mary Shelley wrote a scary story because two guys she was with thought she couldn't write a better one than they could. That scary story was *Frankenstein*. It changed books and literature forever, and we're still reading it and talking about it and marveling over it more than two hundred years later! So to every other weird kid out there: Be like Mary and keep doing your weird things. You just might change the world.

I also firmly believe what Theo told Henry: a nerd is a person who isn't afraid to really love what they love. It's so much fun being a nerd, and I have such an incredible team of really smart, creative, supportive nerds on my side to help me make this series!

At my publisher, Delacorte Press, everyone I work

with is wonderful, but thanks go to my editor, Wendy Loggia, for believing in this series and to Ali Romig, for supporting us both. They help make every single page of these books funnier and more exciting. My publicist, Kristopher Kam, is so good at figuring out how to help readers find the Sinister-Winterbottoms' stories. My stalwart team of copy editors continue to be patiently exasperated with my terrible misuse of hyphens and my love of alliteration. Carol Ly designed these incredible covers, and mad genius Hannah Peck made the absolutely perfect art to go on them. Everyone on the Sinister Team is dedicated and brilliant and an absolute pleasure to work with, and I'm so lucky to be a part of Delacorte Press and Random House Children's Books!

My agent, Michelle Wolfson, really thought I was an extremely normal, calm, not-at-all-spooky person with regular opinions about raisins when we met and started working together more than a dozen years ago. Even though she is often aghast at what I send her, she's always my friend and champion and partner.

My bffs, Natalie Whipple and Stephanie Perkins, would absolutely infiltrate a spooky manor science camp with me to solve mysteries. Actually, that sounds delightful. Let's sign up right now! I also regularly fling drafts at

Stephanie in a panic and ask her to help me make them better, and she always, always does.

None of my stories would have the joy and humor they do if my life wasn't filled with both those things thanks to my husband and my three kids. I feel lucky every day to be a family with my four favorite people in the whole world.

I also feel lucky every day to get to tell stories for a living, so thank you for reading! The Sinister Summer books are the most fun I've ever had writing, and I hope they're as fun to read.

Last, and certainly least, thanks go to Kimberly, who neither knows nor cares that these books exist, does not do anything to help me write them, and is generally useless when it comes to assisting me with my job, because she is a tortoise and cannot read.

ABOUT THE AUTHOR

Kiersten White has never been a seaside amusement park employee, science camp counselor, or churro stand operator, and in fact has never once experienced summer or summer vacation or solved any mysteries during the aforementioned season. Anyone saying otherwise is lying, and you should absolutely not listen to them, even if they offer you a churro. *Especially* if they offer you a churro.

Though she was never a seaside amusement park employee, science camp counselor, or churro stand operator, Kiersten is the *New York Times* bestselling author of more than twenty books, including *Beanstalker and Other Hilarious Scarytales*. She lives with her family near the beach and keeps all her secrets safely buried in her backyard, where they are guarded by a ferocious tortoise named Kimberly.

Visit her at kierstenwhite.com, or check out sinistersummer.com for clues about what awaits the Sinister-Winterbottoms in their next adventure. . . .

JOIN THE SINISTER-WINTERBOTTOM
TWINS IN THEIR LAST ADVENTURE IN

SINISTER SUMMER

HAUNTED HOLIDAY

CHAPTER

CHAPTER ONE

Theo and Alexander Sinister-Winterbottom sat in an impossible place, trying to solve an impossible problem.

Normally, Theo loved word problems. She imagined their current predicament (a word that was fun to say but wasn't fun to experience, because it meant a difficult situation) as a question she might get in math class.

Car A is being driven 62 miles per hour by a man with small mean eyes and a large mean mustache, transporting your sister and all your friends to an unknown location. Car B isn't a car at all, but rather a ghostly aunt who has transported you and your twin brother to her house, which exists not in the real world but somewhere else entirely. How long will it be until you can figure out a way to escape the spectral house and rescue your sister and friends? Show your work!

Theo paced the confines of Aunt Saffronia's tiny kitchen, stepping only on the black tiles. Because Theo had a hard time understanding or explaining her emotions, she always felt like she was filled with bees. Sometimes the bees were quiet and orderly. Sometimes they were busy. Right now, they were a frenzied swarm of chaos and noise, making it impossible to focus. She felt trapped, and she hated feeling trapped. Worse, she felt helpless, and she hated feeling helpless. Worst, people she cared about were in trouble, and she couldn't help them until she figured out how not to be trapped and helpless.

But how could she figure out anything if she was about to explode into a torrent of angry bees? She wished she really *could* explode into bees, because then at least she could fly away after Edgaren't and Essa. Especially Essa, who had pretended to be their friend and then revealed herself to be their ultimate enemy.

If Theo felt trapped, Alexander felt lost. Even though none of this was his fault, Alexander still blamed himself.

If he were an artist, his specialty would be the worst-case scenario—painting every terrible thing that might happen in any given setting. Part of him believed that if he was careful and cautious and always, *always* anticipated what might go wrong, he could see the wrong headed their way and stop it from happening.

But he hadn't seen Essa's betrayal coming. And because he had failed, he'd lost Wil, and Edgar and Quincy and Mina and Lucy and Henry, and even poor Mister Frank. He'd just started trusting himself, but now he didn't know if he should. After all, he'd liked and trusted Essa, and look where that had gotten them.

Alexander stared at the postcard Wil had seen a clue on. But he couldn't figure out what she had discovered. It was only the stamp, the barcode printed on the postcard, a photo of his mom with little Wil and a mystery woman, and a message to Mina and Lucy's dad. But there were no secret words, nothing bolded or italicized, nothing that gave him any hints. It was just a note between old friends.

He had no idea what he was looking at, or even what he was looking for. Possibilities spun in his head over and over, until he felt like a dog chasing its tail. He also hated *that* thought, since he was afraid of most dogs—a fact that embarrassed him, so now he was embarrassed in addition to being anxious and stressed out and sad.

All he'd ever wanted to do was keep himself and the people he loved safe, and he couldn't do that now.

Aunt Saffronia hovered—literally hovered, an inch above the black-and-white tiles—near the fridge, wringing her hands. "I'm sorry," she whispered. "I'm bound to obey Wil's request, since she's the one who summoned me. She told me to keep you safe, so safe is how I must keep you."

"What if you sent us back and we promised to be really, really careful?" Theo asked. "Alexander's super careful!"

Aunt Saffronia shook her head mournfully. "I will not accept a promise I know you cannot keep. If I take you back to the manor, back to Wil and your friends, you will not be safe."

"Can you give us a hint?" Alexander asked. "A way we can get around what Wil asked you to do?"

Their only answer was another sad, ghostly sigh.

"That's okay," Alexander said. He could tell Aunt Saffronia wasn't happy, and even when he was miserable, he was still sensitive to other people's emotions. "It must be hard, being bound by other people's rules."

Theo nodded, a thoughtful tilt to her head. "It is. No one has ever wondered how *I* feel about it."

"I'm sorry," Alexander said.

"I'm sorry, too," Theo grumbled. "I know this isn't your fault." She wasn't good at understanding her own emotions, much less other people's, but she understood this. She hated following arbitrary rules from other people.

Theo slouched at the table, taking a seat next to Alexander as she glared at their pile of stuff. Alexander had taken everything out of his suitcase. Five of the books they'd stolen back from Edgaren't were stacked up and set aside. Alexander gave both the Sinister family book and the Siren family book their own pile, since one was theirs and one had led Wil to a breakthrough. If only she'd told them what she'd discovered before Aunt Saffronia whisked them away from Essa's trap!

"I still can't believe Essa is working with Edgaren't," Alexander said. It made him so, so sad.

"I can't believe it, either," Theo said. It made her so, so mad.

"Can you tell us more about Essa, or what they're doing?" Alexander asked their aunt.

Aunt Saffronia shook her head once more. "The more

you know, the closer you are to danger. I've already put you in too much danger as it is." As though she couldn't bear to be near them without helping, Aunt Saffronia left, or rather, disappeared. One moment she was standing next to the marigold-colored wall in her flowing white dress, and the next moment she wasn't.

"It's too much," Alexander said, despairing. "It's all too much. I don't know why Essa took them, or who she is, or why Edgaren't is working for her, or why she told us the same things Aunt Saffronia did—that we needed time, and to look closer, and to stick together. Or why she's looking for our parents. Or where our parents are. Or who the Sirens are. Or what Wil found in this postcard that solved everything. Or how we'll get out of here. Or even how to get back to Wil and the others if we ever do get out of here."

Theo could tell Alexander was close to crying. While everyone should feel comfortable crying, if that's what they need to do, Theo also knew that crying would give Alexander a headache. She doubted Aunt Saffronia had medicine for headaches, if she hadn't even known children needed food when they first arrived here what felt like months ago.

Their mother always made them tea from her herb garden when they had headaches or felt ill. Theo wished she could do that for Alexander now. Or better yet, she wished that their mom were here and could take care of this mess, and take care of them, too.

"Mom always knew what to do." Theo tipped her head back and ran her fingers through her hair, making it stick up as though she had been electrocuted in that terrible lightning-powered trap Essa created.

"Dad always knew, too," Alexander said. Then he slapped his forehead. "Break it down into pieces!"

"You want to break something?" Theo perked up. She loved breaking things. Her favorite activity at science camp had been the shattering room. But thinking of science camp made her think of Essa again. Theo perked down.

"No, not that. Whenever we have word problems we can't solve, Dad helps us break them down into parts, right? Or when we help him build his battle robots. He doesn't build a whole robot at once."

"He tackles it piece by piece!" Theo nodded, getting excited.

"We've been looking at the problem as a whole: how

do we get out of here and save everyone we care about and find our parents. But that's overwhelming—it's too much at once. Let's break it down into parts."

"Right! First, we need to figure out how to get out of here." Theo resumed pacing, but this time it was to help herself think. If her body was moving, it helped her brain move, too. "If we were building a robot with Dad—"

"Or solving a word problem—"

"He'd have us look at what we already have to work with."

Alexander ticked things off on his fingers. "We have the books. We have Mom's letter to us. We have the postcard from the Siren book, where Wil saw a clue."

"We have the objects we've found." Theo took off her timer and set it in the center of the table. Alexander added his magnifying glass and Wil's toothless key.

"What are our resources in Aunt Saffronia's house?" Alexander asked.

Theo looked around the kitchen. "The fridge. So we have food, and aren't in an emergency situation there. That phone thingie, I guess? The table and chairs, but we can't use them to bust our way out of here. The windows aren't real and there's no door." Theo had tried running out of the kitchen, but every time she stepped through the doorway, she found herself right back in the middle of the tile floor. In other circumstances it might actually have been fun, but today it was super aggravating.

"And Aunt Saffronia herself could be a resource, if we can find a way around her rules. Okay, so this is what we have to work with." Alexander frowned, deep in thought. "But how do we use these things to get back to the real world?"

"You forgot two resources," Theo said.

Alexander looked up, puzzled. "What are they?"

Theo sat once more, taking his hand. "Us. We're Theo and Alexander Sinister-Winterbottom. We're brave and careful, and we're kind, helpful friends, and we're *great* at solving mysteries."

Alexander smiled at last, Theo's confidence in them making his despair melt away. He might not have been able to protect everyone alone, but they would be able to do it together. He was sure of it. "We're the most important part of the equation."

"Exactly." Theo's bees calmed down. Whatever was ahead of them, however long it took, she knew: they were going to solve every problem that came their way, together. "You can always call on me for help."

"That's it!" Alexander shouted, standing. "Theo, you're a genius!"

"I am!" Theo agreed. Then she paused. "I am?"

Alexander's smile was so bright it practically glowed. "I know exactly how we're getting out of here. What's my favorite thing?"

"Safely prepared food."

Alexander laughed. "Second-favorite thing."

"Clearly defined rules so you know exactly how to follow them."

"Third-favorite—"

"Matching socks. The Magnificent English Confectionary Challenge. Puzzles. Reading on rainy days. Me. Warm cookies. When you wake up just a few minutes before your alarm, so you get to snuggle in and—"

Alexander interrupted her. "Adult supervision," he said. "Because it makes everything . . ."

"Safe!" Theo shouted. "That's it! We just have to find an adult to supervise us, and then we'll have filled the requirements of Wil's demand, so Aunt Saffronia will be able to let us go." Theo paused, and her spirits fell once more. "But what adult? We don't know where Mom and Dad are. Essa has Wil, and she's not really an adult anyway, even if she thinks she is. Who else can we ask for help? And *how* can we ask them?"

"I can think of a few people we've helped lately who would be willing to help us now. And as to the last question . . ."

Alexander collected many things: cool rocks, new words, recipes, phobias, and, most unusually for a kid his age, *phone numbers*. He pointed to Aunt Saffronia's telephone. "We're going to call."